THE BOY WHO RETURNED
FROM THE SEA

THE BOY WHO RETURNED FROM THE SEA

Clay Morgan

DUTTON CHILDREN'S BOOKS

DUTTON CHILDREN'S BOOKS
A division of Penguin Young Readers Group

Published by the Penguin Group
Penguin Group (USA) Inc., 375 Hudson Street, New York, New York 10014, U.S.A. • Penguin
Group (Canada), 90 Eglinton Avenue East, Suite 700, Toronto, Ontario, Canada M4P 2Y3 (a
division of Pearson Penguin Canada Inc.) • Penguin Books Ltd, 80 Strand, London WC2R oRL,
England • Penguin Ireland, 25 St Stephen's Green, Dublin 2, Ireland (a division of Penguin Books
Ltd) • Penguin Group (Australia), 250 Camberwell Road, Camberwell, Victoria 3124, Australia
(a division of Pearson Australia Group Pty Ltd) • Penguin Books India Pvt Ltd, 11 Community
Centre, Panchsheel Park, New Delhi - 110 017, India • Penguin Group (NZ), 67 Apollo Drive,
Rosedale, North Shore 0745, Auckland, New Zealand (a division of Pearson New Zealand Ltd) •
Penguin Books (South Africa) (Pty) Ltd, 24 Sturdee Avenue, Rosebank, Johannesburg 2196, South
Africa • Penguin Books Ltd, Registered Offices: 80 Strand, London WC2R oRL, England

The publisher does not have any control over and does not assume any responsibility for author
or third-party websites or their content.

CIP Data is available.

Published in the United States by Dutton Children's Books,
a division of Penguin Young Readers Group
345 Hudson Street, New York, New York 10014
www.penguin.com/youngreaders
Designed by Jason Henry

Printed in USA * First Edition
ISBN 978-0-525-47401-2
2 4 6 8 10 9 7 5 3 1

For Moxie

THE BOY WHO RETURNED
FROM THE SEA

I

Moxie, the little Border collie, stood on the sea cliffs. She whimpered and looked out over the wide, wild ocean. She lifted her nose and opened her mouth, panting to get some news from the breeze.

From the sea, she was hoping. *From the sea—*

Someday her boy would return from the sea. Her boy, Jack, would come back to this wilderness island, which had sheep dogs and sheep, but not any humans.

Moxie sniffed the evening air. She smelled seawater, sea salt, seaweed, and fishes. She smelled the crusty sand drying in the sun. She smelled the cast-about seashells bleaching to white, and the crabby seagulls, squabbling over food. When the gulls flapped their wings, Moxie smelled their ruffling feathers. But she did not smell her boy.

She could smell that it was midday. It was summer again. The weather would continue warm and fair. This much was good. But there was much that was wrong. Moxie could smell her own hunger.

She smelled it on her own breath. It was a sour stomach smell, acid and anxious. It burned her nose and tightened her throat. The smell reminded Moxie that she and the other hungry sheep dogs needed to eat something, soon.

Moxie sneezed, to get the hunger smell out of her nose. She sneezed, and she sneezed again. Then she sniffed the breeze, but still she could not smell her boy.

Her breathing shortened. Her heart skipped a beat. Her head dropped low. *She missed Jack!* She felt a hunger for food, a hunger for Jack, and a hunger for what it means to be a dog.

Moxie sighed and shivered. She watched the seagulls below her on the beach. They spread their wings. They hopped into the air. They flew. They rose, to sail above her on the wind. The gulls soared high, without strain or effort. But as easy as this was for them, they squawked and they cried. Moxie thought they had nothing really to complain about. Why? Because they were birds. Birds had wings. Birds could fly. They could see far.

Maybe they could see Jack?

Moxie strained to see him, too, out on the ocean. Where? Where? Where had Jack gone?

She panted and sighed. She almost whined. Feeling weak and sad, she padded down through the sheep meadow to the green swale where Jack had once built a shelter, when he had lived on the island with her.

When she got to the shelter, Moxie began digging into the dirt, to sniff for a fading memory of Jack. She dug and sniffed for some scent that would bring back his laughter. To Moxie, Jack's laughter had always sounded like wild, happy barking.

2

But at that very moment, Jack wasn't laughing. Instead, he felt like he should be crying. He was standing at the rail of the tramp steamer named *Pym*, in front of its big paddle wheel, which was beating at the ocean.

The rusty old *Pym* was churning through the waves, just off the coast of New Zealand's North Island. Slowly, the *Pym* was towing a raft of huge kauri logs. They were to be made into lumber at a sawmill near Auckland.

As its paddle wheel splashed, the *Pym* shuddered and chugged. It was working its way through a big sunny bay filled with green wooded islands. Surely, Moxie was on one of the islands. But on which one? On that one? Or that one? Or—?

Which one was Moxie's? Which one was Dog Island?

It had been one year now, since he and Moxie had last seen each other—since Jack's friends Cookie and the two Maori sailors, Tanati and Toa, had come back to the island to rescue Jack.

But it hadn't felt like a rescue to Jack.

On that day, his friends surprised Jack on the beach. When he had tried to run, they grabbed him. He fought them so fiercely that they thought he had gone wild. But they dragged him into their rowboat and held him tight. Then they tried to catch Moxie, but she was too quick. They had to leave her on the beach, frantically barking. Jack's friends rowed Jack back to a ship, away from his life with the dogs, and back into the world of humans.

For Jack, the year away had felt like he was living inside someone else's life. Now he leaned over the *Pym*'s rail and he strained to see better.

Is it that island? he wondered. *Or that one? Or that one?*

3

Indeed, Moxie was on an island, some miles in front of the *Pym*. She lingered on the cliff top, watching the sea for Jack. She missed him as only a dog can miss a boy, longing to smell his boy smell again.

Just then, Moxie heard a drumming. Something was running straight at her. She flinched. She thought, *Oh! Not again!*

Then *slam!* Moxie was struck broadside. She went rolling through the grass. She struggled to her feet, and she barely hopped out of the way as a blur of speckled fur *whooshed* right past her.

The blur was black, white, and brown. It was furry and fast. It was a speeding and furry *blur*.

In fact, Blur was this furry blur's name. Blur was a young and happy Australian shepherd pup. Right now, Blur was spraying grass and dirt out behind him. He carved a tight turn so he could rush back at Moxie and bump her again.

But Blur tripped on a tussock. That sent him tumbling. *Kalumitpy-thump.* And it stopped him, still.

For a moment, Blur lay flat on his back, panting, with his tongue hanging out. He regarded Moxie, from upside down.

"Good day!" he greeted her.

His happiness made Moxie's tail wag, by itself. Blur was all dash and flash, and, usually, crash. Blur had energy that none of the other dogs had, anymore. The other dogs all wondered where he got his vigor, but Blur was too happy to wonder about himself.

"Happy up!" he would tell Moxie. "Let's jump up an adventure!"

Blur rarely stopped pestering Moxie, except when he was chasing his shadows. He was too happy to be helpful, and too carefree to be careful.

Now Blur was smiling an upside-down smile. His tongue hung from his mouth, across his left eye.

He slobbered. "What's the matter, Moxie? What worries?" He obviously thought there was no need to worry.

"It's all worries!" Moxie said to him, sternly now. "Everything is worries."

But she couldn't help liking Blur. Blur was a ray of canine sunshine.

"Happy up!" Blur said, upside down. "Come on! Race me! Chase me! Let's jump! Let's run! Let's tear something up!"

Blur rolled over, to sit upright, and he tore at a grass tussock with his teeth.

"Let's settle down," Moxie told him. "Let's grow up, a little."

Blur laughed a quick, happy pant.

"Grow up?" he said. "Too soon. Too soon. First let's get up some fun."

He faked a charge at Moxie.

"Made you jump!" Blur laughed, and he started jumping.

"Aren't you hungry?" Moxie asked.

That stopped him. "Oh!" Blur remembered. "Oh! Now! So hungry!"

Confusion crossed his eyes. But then a new thought came into them as he looked out over the ocean.

"Birds!" he said.

"Oh, no. Not birds," Moxie said. "Not the birds, again."

"Birds!" Blur shouted.

And he was gone, in a blur.

Blur raced to the edge of the cliff, where he skidded to a stop. He stood, stock-still, and put his nose to the ground. He began wagging his tail, in a whir.

Moxie padded closer to him. Blur's birds game was funny, but it was almost painful to watch.

It was also sometimes painful to Blur.

Blur played his game like this. After he got into position on the cliff top, he looked out over the ocean, to see if any gulls were riding the winds. Today, the gulls were out there. They were riding the winds at the level of the cliff tops. The soaring gulls flew facing out to the ocean, gliding left and right.

"Birds!" Blur exclaimed. "Birds! Birds!"

Then Blur turned away from the gulls, to face in the direction of the meadow. He put his nose low near the ground and he stood still, but quivering.

"Birds!" he said, but didn't watch the birds. He watched the ground, as he quivered. His tail was wagging almost too fast to see. Blur was a blur, even standing still.

Moxie got ready for what she knew would happen. Blur stood, all abuzz and aquiver, his tail fanning fast, his nose to the ground. Out over the ocean, one of the gulls tipped a wing and wheeled around, and began a wide swoop, coming back toward the cliff top.

As she watched the gull sail toward them, Moxie winced in anticipation. She said, "Be more careful this time, Blur!"

Her warning made Blur all the more excited. He watched the ground, all buzzing.

"B-b-b-b-birds!" he buzzed.

The seagull swooped toward them, toward the cliff's edge. As it sailed overhead, the gull's shadow crossed the cliff top, then flashed through the grass. When Blur saw the shadow, he dashed after it.

Zoom! Blur chased the bird shadow as it zipped through the bushes and tussocks. Blur raced right behind it, running full tilt. He chased. He sprinted. He sped. He dodged. He stumbled, and recovered. He blasted through the tussocks and the brush and the bushes.

Moxie watched. Blur was so fast! So quick! So amazing!

Until—

Oh, no, Moxie thought. *Here it comes.*

And once again—

Ka-wham!

Blur ran straight into one of the big rocks.

Fahlump! He fell to the ground like a bag full of clods.

Moxie winced.

Then she sighed. She trotted down to Blur, and she sat on her haunches beside him.

Blur looked like he was sleeping. He was knocked out, cold. But as always, Blur looked like he was happy. Moxie envied him, even when he was unconscious.

Then one of Blur's legs began to twitch. Then all four of his legs began to move, as if he was chasing birds in his dreams.

In his dreams, Blur ran, he jumped, he dodged.

Zip! Zap! Zoom!

Then—*wham!*—Blur jerked hard, and fell still.

Moxie wondered if Blur had just hit a rock in his dream.

She watched him. What a life this goofy pup led.

After some seconds, Blur opened his eyes. He sat up.

He shook his head. He blinked. He blinked again. His eyes were not focusing on the same point.

Slowly Blur regained himself. His tongue came out. He began his happy pant.

"Birds?" he asked Moxie. His eyebrows went up.

Moxie smiled and nodded. She liked Blur. Sometimes he helped her forget.

An iron door suddenly clanged open behind Jack. He turned just in time to see a wiry little man come flying out through a hatch. The little man slammed against the deck railing. He bounced off, and fell to the deck. The railing kept thrumming a low wobbly rumble, like a drumroll introducing a circus act.

The little man rolled over onto his back. He rolled his head back and forth.

"*Uhhhh—*" he said. "*Uhhhh—*"

The little man wore cut-off dungarees and a torn woolen jersey with red and white stripes. His face was haggard. His eyes were pinched closed, his lips clamped tight. He rolled his head back and forth on the deck.

Then his eyes popped open. The sight of them made

Jack jump back. They were strange eyes. They looked empty, almost ghostly, and yet they held something inside them. Jack peered more closely. The little man's eyes were a smoky, glassy gray. But what was it that Jack saw in them?

It was Jack's own reflection.

"What on—?" Jack began to say. He leaned in, to look closer. *What on earth—?* Was this man blind?

Then the little man blinked, and Jack jumped back again.

But the man could not see. Or could he? As a test, Jack moved silently to his right.

The man's craggy face followed him.

But how? Jack wondered.

"That's how!" the little man said. "Yes, I am blind, if you look at it *that* way."

His eyes closed. Then they popped back open. "But let us say this. Let us say that I look for new ways to look."

The little man nodded, one certain nod. "And—So—Shall—You!"

He blinked in a way that made Jack blink, too.

The wiry little man turned his face back toward the open hatch, out of which he had recently flown.

"Well?" he said to someone, inside the ship. "Well? Come on! Come out! What took you?"

Then a great roar rolled out through the hatchway.

"ARRRHHH!!!"

Jack's ears cringed. It was the roar of Cap'n Gully.

"ARRRHHH!!!" Big Cap'n Gully pulled himself through the hatchway, with both hands. As he did so, he began to curse down at the little man on the deck.

He cursed the purplest words Jack had ever heard. They were the loudest words, too, all splattered out in Gully's ear-curdling voice.

"You fool and you fowlard! You bum and you blow-fly! You festering, filthering, fulsome pest!"

Cap'n Gully's eyes flared, full of fire and bloodshot. His red eyebrows looked as though he had slept on them for days, and then had rubbed them in circles with hack-up and spit.

His eyebrows quivered. "You low-down, bottom-feeding, rotten-roe ratbag!" he swore at the little blind man.

The little man listened politely. Then he worked up a grin, and flashed it at Cap'n Gully.

"Now and now," the little man said. "Such and such."

He shook his smile. "It won't help us none to call us bad names."

Cap'n Gully gurgled. *"Rrrgghh!"* He pressed his shut eyes with the heels of his hands. "You bush piker! Beach ranger! Swag-loving scum!"

Gully jackhammered his fat finger down at the blind man in stripes. Then he used the worst name of all. He thundered, "You *DIGGER!* You *stowaway DIGGER!*"

Unabashed, the little blind man sat up. He brushed off his sleeves. He said, "I am here because of Blackburn Jukes."

Cap'n Gully's eyes flared.

Jack cringed.

This wouldn't be pretty.

5

Watching Blur had made Moxie feel good for a moment. But she needed to do something that would make her feel even better.

Moxie left the cliff top, and trotted down through the high meadow to a place where Jack had built one of his rock shelters. There, Moxie started digging for a scent memory of Jack. She dug up pebbles and roots. She dug up dirt and sand. Finally, she found one rusty spoon.

Moxie stopped when she found the spoon. A spoon was a human thing. But as she sniffed at it, it made her feel worse.

This spoon came from the far old days, from before Jack had first come to the island. The spoon had no human scent left on it. It gave off only a rough and buzzy, faintly ringing smell of rust. To a dog, rust smells like the air during a lightning storm, except older, like after the electricity that has died.

This rusty spoon smelled way too dead. Still, Moxie took up the spoon in her mouth. She trotted with it to the place by the old rock wall where she kept all the human things she found.

Moxie dropped the spoon onto her small pile of human things. In the pile, there were also a hatchet and two other spoons. There were also a knife, several nails, and a closed tin box.

This box smelled wonderful to Moxie. It smelled of pipe tobacco and Jack. Although she could not open the box, she knew it held memories. Moxie knew it held things that had been important to Jack.

Before Jack had come to the island, the box had belonged to the pipe-smoking humans in the far old days. The old sheep dog Sage had told Moxie about them. And when Jack had been on the island, he had treasured it and held it to his cheek. That was how the box had picked up Jack's scent.

Moxie sniffed again at the box. She sniffed it, deeply. Sadly, it, too, was beginning to smell more of rust.

With half a heart, Moxie started digging again. To

her surprise, a new scent touched her hunger. It charged her, and made her dig faster.

This smell wasn't a human's scent. Instead, it was the odor of a vole—a warm little mouse creature with a stubby tail. Moxie smelled that the vole was close to her, barely underground. Moxie could hear that it was tunneling away.

Moxie dug faster. Dirt sprayed between her hind legs. She dug, she sniffed, and she dug.

Then she nipped.

Snap! She caught the vole by one leg with the tips of her front teeth. The vole wiggled to get free, but Moxie tossed it up into the air. She caught it, whole, in her mouth.

Moxie's hungry throat wanted to swallow the vole whole. Her throat tried to gulp it, but she could not let it. This meal was not for her. It was for Mother Molly and her puppies.

Moxie resisted as her throat pulled downward, trying again to swallow the vole. She was so hungry. *So hungry.* Her stomach pleaded. But Moxie did not swallow the vole. Instead, she trotted down toward another of Jack's old shelters, where the mother dog Molly kept her litter of puppies.

Think of the puppies, Moxie kept saying to herself. *Always think of the pups.*

But as she trotted, the vole squirmed and wiggled on the back of her tongue. The vole squirmed. Moxie's saliva flowed. *Oh—!* Her stomach begged.

The vole squirmed harder. Moxie stopped trotting. This was too hard. The vole was squirming on her tongue. Moxie squeezed shut her throat and did her best to resist it.

But then the little vole touched that one spot on the back of Moxie's tongue that always made her throat go *Ga-lulp!*

And *Ga-lulp!* Moxie swallowed the vole, whole and entire.

Ga-lulp? Moxie thought. *Oh, no!*

Moxie had two feelings, one right after the other. First her stomach rejoiced because food was inside it. Then she felt a horrible guilt for letting down Molly's puppies. She had swallowed the vole. Oh, it felt good. But she had failed the puppies.

Moxie felt like slinking away—to go roll in something rotten, to slime herself in shame.

But a stronger instinct made her start padding toward the puppies again.

Soon she was trotting.

Then she was running.

She ran as fast as she could.

Moxie arrived at Jack's old shelter. Inside it lay Molly, with her pups at her side. The puppies were too young to be able to see. They nosed their mother's belly for milk. They were something to behold. They were little dog lives, tiny and furry.

Moxie and Molly touched noses.

"I am sorry," Moxie said.

"Sorry for what?" Molly asked.

Moxie could only shake her head.

But then an instinct made Moxie lean down to the pups. The puppies began to lick Moxie on her nose. They all licked her nose, and all the licking caused Moxie's stomach to twist and squeeze, tight.

Suddenly, up came the vole that she had just swallowed. It came up through Moxie's throat. It landed, wet and squirming, right in front of Molly.

In a wink, Molly snapped it up and swallowed.

"Ah!" she said. "Thank you! Thank you, Moxie!"

"What?" Moxie wondered. "How did that happen?"

"The puppies licked your nose," Molly said.

Moxie put her nose down to the puppies again. Sure

enough, when they licked her nose, her stomach tried to bring up more food.

"That's how it happens," Molly said. "And now I will make milk, and nurse my puppies."

"That's a wonder," Moxie said.

But what is *wonder*? Is wonder the hunger to know? Moxie felt hunger in her belly, and in her mind, and in her heart. She hungered to know how to help the sheep dogs survive. She hungered to know when Jack was coming home.

6

Jack watched as Cap'n Gully gritted his smile into a grimace. It made him look happy and angry at the same time. He wiped the back of his hand across his tongue. The taste made him shake his big head and spit.

He said to the little blind man, "You are the third stowaway we've caught, this week, who has blurted the name of Blackburn Jukes. *Blazes!* How can one man have such a reputation among diggers?"

The little man spread his hands, in a show of explanation. He said, "Blackburn Jukes knows the bog. Blackburn Jukes knows the bog gum. It be said that Blackburn Jukes knows how to use the buzz!"

"Bog gum?" Cap'n Gully repeated. "*Buzz?*"

Then Gully shook his head, to get rid of these thoughts. He looked back into the hatchway.

He sang out, "Oh, boys!"

"Aye, Cap'n," came a voice.

"Aye, Cap'n," came another.

The two voices sounded almost like they had come from the same man. But two sailors squeezed through the hatchway, together. They were red-faced, blond-haired, round-headed Australians.

Cap'n Gully commanded them, "Overboard with this digger!"

"Aye, Cap'n," said both Pete and Jon.

But neither did anything but cross his arms.

Cap'n Gully roared at them. "Do it now!"

"Aye, Cap'n," said Pete.

Pete nodded to Jon. Jon nodded back at Pete, and then nodded to Jack. Jack looked at Gully for his reaction.

Gully's eye whites were already bloodied up, red. He choked out a gurgle that sounded like a threat.

That made Pete raise his hand. "We understand, Cap'n," Pete said.

Then Pete lowered his hand. "And yet—"

Pete didn't finish. He put his hand to his chin.

Jon spoke for him. "And yet—" Jon said. "And yet,

you look here. I believe this here digger is technically, medically *bloind*."

Cap'n Gully looked as though he was about to swallow his tongue. But he recovered, and he made fun of Jon's accent. "*Buh-loind? Did I hear someone say 'buh-loind'?*"

"I said it," Jon said. He didn't realize that Gully was mocking him.

"He did say it," Pete agreed. Pete didn't get Gully's joke, either. "Jon did say it. And Jon meant it. Jon meant to say '*bloind.*'"

"Aye, right," Jon said. "This man here is *bloind*. And we'd rather not drown a *bloind* man who cannot see."

Suddenly curious, Cap'n Gully asked them, "And why would you not?"

Pete and Jon did not seem to know.

Cap'n Gully shook his big head. He pinched his fat cheek with his big hand. Then he reached down and picked up the little man by the collar of his striped sweater. He hoisted him, one-handed, off the ship's deck.

"No!" Jack said. He heard the loud splashing of the paddle wheel behind him.

The little man coughed. The neck of his sweater was choking him. He coughed, but still he didn't look frightened. As he twisted slowly, he looked at Jack with his blind, gray eyes.

"Jack!" he choked out. "Learn to look, Jack. Learn to look—"

Jack interrupted. "You called me Jack!"

The little man coughed. "Every boy is Jack."

"He is?" asked Jack.

The little man touched his own ear, and then one eye, and then pointed his finger at Jack.

"Learn to look—" he started.

But he choked as Cap'n Gully twisted his collar more tightly.

Gully held out the little man to Pete and Jon. "Here, you take him. You toss him. Throw him overboard."

"Aye," they both said, and nodded.

Jack protested. "No!"

But Pete and Jon put their hands into the little man's armpits.

"No!" Jack shouted.

And as easily as though the little man were a pail of slopped garbage, Pete and Jon began swinging the little man back and forth.

"No!" Jack shouted.

The sailors started laughing. Cap'n Gully tried not to laugh.

"NO!" Jack shouted.

But Pete and Jon were laughing, swinging the little man between them. Then they launched the little blind man up and out. He sailed out over the *Pym's* deck railing.

The little blind man flew. Jack watched with horror as the little man's arms rowed like oars. He turned two and a half somersaults over the ocean. His red-and-white-striped sweater flapped like an American flag. Then— *ker-ploomk!*—he plopped into a billow of the sea, making a hole in the water, which was pitifully brief.

Jack winced. *Ker-ploomk?* Would that be all for this man? Just to go *plunk* and to sink away?

But, no! The man rose to the surface, like a cork. He spit out water in a stream, and began to slap at the waves around him.

Jack watched in horror. Could the little man swim?

It didn't look like he could.

But he didn't look too concerned about it, either. He was facing toward Jack. He shook his head as though he had just woken up.

"Learn to listen!" he shouted.

That made no sense to Jack. He glanced back along the ship's side. The big paddle wheel was churning toward the little man in the water. It would soon be upon him, and would beat him down under the waves.

Jack waved both his hands, and pointed toward the approaching side-wheel.

"Hey, hey!" Jack shouted. "Hey! Hey! Swim!"

"Listen!" the man shouted back.

"SWIM!" Jack screamed.

"To the gum bog!" the man shouted.

To the gum bog? Jack wondered.

Next to Jack at the rail, Cap'n Gully was now laughing with his two sailors.

And below Jack in the ocean, the little man did start swimming.

He started stroking quite nicely, all things considered. But instead of swimming away from the ship, he swam alongside it, with the ship's big paddle wheel approaching, *slap-slap-slapping* toward him.

"No!" Jack shouted.

For a few milling strokes, the little man kept pace with the *Pym*.

"Look at him," remarked Jon. "I believe that this fellow is swimming the famed 'Australian crawl.'"

"He is!" Pete agreed. "And he's doing quite well."

Cap'n Gully crossed his arms. "This *Pym* is too slow," he complained. "Someday, I'll have me a ship with propellers."

But the big paddle wheel was now catching up on the little man in the striped jersey.

"HEY!" Jack shouted down at him. "Swim AWAY from the ship! SWIM AWAY from my voice!"

Amazingly, the little man turned and swam away.

The paddle wheel missed him, just barely. It *slap-slap-slap-slap-slapped* past him.

Jack let go a huge sigh of release.

Pete asked his mate, "Would you look at that, Jon?"

"I would. It's the luck of the diggers, Pete. Don't you know? It goes to show, as you already know. It's as they always say. You can't drown a rat."

"Wait a minute. No," Pete disagreed. "It's a cat you can't drown."

The two men began a debate. Jack pushed through them, and ran back along the rail, after the little blind man in the ocean. Jack ran toward the stern. He sprinted around windlasses and capstans. He bounded up and down two sets of iron stairs, to get over the sponson and paddle wheel.

At the ship's stern, Jack caught up with the little man in the ocean. He was now floating back into the greasy bilge slick. The little blind man treaded water, rotated slowly in the dirty gray eddy of foam. He was grinning again.

Jack had to grin, too. He knew he was not in danger, anymore. Things would soon get better for the wiry little blind man in stripes. He would float back to the raft of kauri logs, which the *Pym* was towing toward Auckland. The tow raft already had on it a dozen stowaway diggers. They were amber diggers, on their ways to and from the amber mines.

And these diggers were ready. They helped the little man climb out of the sea.

Their raft was made from eight huge kauri logs, chained together. Some of the logs were eight feet wide and eighty feet long. The majestic kauri trees were being cut down nearly everywhere, on many of the islands and on the big North Island mainland.

On board the raft rode the troop of stowaway diggers. The diggers lived like hobos, careless and free. They were riding the kauri raft to Auckland and their next jobs, digging up the buried kauri amber.

7

Moxie left Mother Molly at the shelter with her puppies. She passed through the top of the meadow, where a few hungry sheep dogs guarded the flock of raggedy sheep.

Tram and Boffo were there. Blur was not. Cam was not. Other sheep dogs were gone, too. Perhaps they had shaded up, under some brush, too hungry and too weak to stand. Tram and Boffo did not even look at Moxie. They had stopped asking, "What do we do?" Life for the sheep dogs couldn't be much worse.

The thought of *worse* made Moxie turn to scan the line of trees below her for a sign of what had always been worse—the dire and dreaded fangos.

The fangos were wild things who had once been good

sheep dogs. Until a few weeks before, the fangos used to attack the sheep, often. But Moxie saw no fangos today. Were the fangos as weak as the sheep dogs were?

Moxie did not know. She knew that the fangos were still dangerous and sly. But the fangos were gone today, and Moxie almost missed them.

On Moxie's island, the sheep dogs and the fangos had been living in a weird, life-and-death balance. It was all due to the fact that a true sheep dog must guard sheep as if her soul depended on it.

But a fango would kill a sheep, every chance he got. And so, because the sheep dogs could not kill sheep for themselves to eat, they depended on the fangos to attack the sheep—and then to leave behind some meat.

Many years before, long before Jack had first arrived on the island, there were humans on the island who raised the sheep for their food. Of course, they shared the meat with the sheep dogs. But when the humans disappeared, there was no food for the sheep dogs. They got hungrier and hungrier, until one day when some of the dogs snapped. They slaughtered some sheep and ate them, but by doing so, they lost their dog souls.

There was a great war among the dogs, which the true sheep dogs won. The true sheep dogs banished the bad dogs, who then became the fangos. Losing all their no-bility and self-respect, the fangos became mangy, snarl-ing, slinking low curs, who would attack whenever they could.

During almost every attack, the fangos would drive off a sheep. But they often left behind a wounded and dying sheep, which then became the food for the sheep dogs.

And so, as strange as it was, the sheep dogs had come to depend on the fangos for their food. The sheep dogs knew that they, themselves, could never kill sheep and remain true dogs. So, even as they fought the fangos, it was the fangos who fed them.

As Moxie padded to the meadow, she kept scanning the tree line. It disturbed her, to wish that she would see fangos.

8

Almost every day, Cap'n Gully had caught another digger stowaway. He always ordered Pete and Jon to throw the diggers overboard. So far, all had survived, and all had climbed onto the tow raft of logs.

There they thrived. The diggers turned the log raft into their floating camp. They pitched a large tent made from a salvaged sail. They built a rough wood table and two long plank benches. The diggers kept a cheerful driftwood cook fire going. It burned right on top of one of the floating logs.

Now they crowded around the little blind man. They slapped him on his back. They led him, dripping, to the fire, where he was treated as a hero.

Jack laughed as he watched. He wished that he was

on the raft with them, instead of working as the galley boy for his old friend Cookie.

Jack's old friend Cookie had gotten them the jobs on the *Pym*. It was to keep them going until their skipper, Captain Day, found himself a new ship to command. It would not be until then, Cookie said, that Jack could get back to Moxie's island.

But now Jack ignored the stinking, groaning *Pym*. He admired the diggers on their raft. Two of the men were now dancing a jig. Their knees bobbed up and down. Their elbows jerked back and forth. They threw back their heads and hollered and laughed.

Jack could not hear them. But he saw happiness in the men's sunburned smiles and friendly, squint eyes. Jack laughed with the diggers.

Then he laughed again. He almost barked, but stopped himself, and smiled.

Jack turned away from the raft, to watch the passing islands. At the moment, they looked like green hills on the blue plain of the sea.

Far off, behind the islands, a storm was approaching. Its high, white cloud looked like a sailing ship—like a pirate ship, sailing Jack's way. Was it coming his way? Jack hoped so. Storms change more than the weather.

Storms sometimes change people's lives. It had been a great and sudden storm that had cast Jack onto the beach of Moxie's island, one year before.

Just imagine! Jack thought. Jack shaped his fists into imaginary binoculars. He squinted through them to scan the shores of the passing islands. Was Moxie on that island? Or on that one? Or on that one, there?

Jack focused his hand binoculars on one island that looked promising. Then he squeezed his hands tight, he closed his eyes, and he looked deep into his past. He remembered throwing sticks in the meadow, for Moxie.

9

Moxie's memory worked differently than Jack's did. Because she was a dog, she remembered with her nose.

When she got to Jack's old shelter, she dug and dug. Suddenly, she found a scent.

It was Jack's scent! It was a year old, but it was still warm with his feeling. Moxie scratched into the scent. She sniffed and she snorted, as a memory began to form in her mind of the day she discovered Jack.

In this scent memory, Moxie was down at the beach. She suddenly happened upon a footprint in the sand. How strange it was. How odd and evocative. Then, suddenly, she saw a strange, hairless creature coming toward her. It tottered on its hind legs, waving its front paws. The creature terrified Moxie. She ran away—off the beach, into the forest, right past the fangos, and up to the high meadow.

At that time, one year ago, Moxie had run straight back to old Sage. Sage was the blind English sheep dog who often told the young sheep dogs his memories of the human times. Sage listened to Moxie. He told her that this new creature was not a monster, but one of the humans. A human had returned to Dog Island!

That human had been Jack. Wonderful Jack.

Now Moxie dug deeper, scraping at the earth for more memories.

10

On the tramp steamer *Pym*, it was now late afternoon. Jack turned away from the kauri raft, and started toward the galley. Cookie would be needing him, to help make Cap'n Gully's supper.

On his way, Jack neared an old lifeboat, hanging crooked from its davits. As he passed the boat, he thought he heard a faint, buzzy humming. What was that? Was it wind through some cables?

But the humming was the kind that fills up one's head. Jack stopped and listened. He felt a buzzing in his teeth.

Then he heard a sound—a *sl-sl-thump!*—come from inside the lifeboat.

What's this? he thought. Another digger stowaway?

Jack wanted to peek under the lifeboat's tarp, but he

didn't. It almost made him smile. He wondered how long it would be, before Cap'n Gully discovered this stowaway, too.

So Jack laughed out loud. He wanted whoever was inside the boat to know that at least Jack knew about him. Jack knew that Cap'n Gully didn't pay attention to lifeboats. Judging from this lifeboat's condition—its cracked and bowing planks—Jack figured it couldn't float for very long.

But wait. Maybe it would float. The thought stowed away in his mind. Jack thumped his knuckles against the side of the boat. He wondered, if he could take an old lifeboat like this and slip away from the ship, could he go and search the islands for Moxie?

Maybe the boat wouldn't leak too bad. Or it wouldn't spring a gusher, anyway. Jack could hoist up one oar, and rig the tarpaulin as a sail. He could steer the boat by using the other oar as a rudder. Jack could sail this entire, vast bay of islands, and find that one good island with his true dog, Moxie.

Hmm. Now, yes! That was a plan. Yes, it was.

But then something went *shlump!* inside the lifeboat again. The tarpaulin lifted, and two dark eyes peered out.

Startled, Jack hurried away from it, toward the galley.

Moxie dug for more memories.

She dug. She sniffed. She dug. She sniffed. She caught a scent. What was this?

It wasn't Jack. It was another odor. It was very faint, but it was real, and amazing. *Oh, my!* It was the scent of brave Kelso, the late leader of the sheep dogs. Kelso had died in the big battle with the fangos, just before Jack was taken away.

Moxie sniffed up all of Kelso's scent. Then she sat back on her haunches and let its vapor fill up her brain. As it did, a vision of Kelso appeared in her mind. Kelso was a big German shepherd, with broad shoulders.

Be vigilant, Moxie! Kelso's vision said, inside her mind.

But we're hungry, Moxie thought. *We're weak. We haven't eaten. What do we do? How do we eat?*

Protect the sheep, Kelso's vision said. *Be vigilant, Moxie.*

We are vigilant, Moxie thought. *But the fangos have stopped attacking. We have no food without the fangos. So what do we do? What do we do?*

Be vigilant, said Kelso, again. *Be vigilant. Be vigilant. Be . . .*

And Kelso's voice faded with his vision of him.

Moxie shook her head. That had not helped. She started to dig again. Deeper, she smelled another scent. This was the scent of blind old Sage.

Moxie inhaled it, and a vision of Sage appeared in her mind. She saw wise, old Sage, with his fringe of white hair hanging down over his blind eyes.

Hello, dear Moxie, Sage said. *How are you?*

Moxie's mind blurted, *Sage! What do we do?*

Sage's vision faded. But then it revived.

Sage said, *Moxie, you must search. You must look where you haven't looked. You must find what you have never seen. And learn.*

Moxie didn't understand this. She asked, *What? What do you mean?*

12

Jack found his old friend Cookie in the galley, flouring a breadboard. The old man's face and forearms were floured white. So was his smooth bald head. And so was Cookie's wonderful, single white eyebrow, which grew clear across the bridge of his nose.

Cookie always smiled when he saw Jack. When he smiled, his eyebrow, too, was shaped like a smile.

The old man beamed. "There you are, Jackie Tar!"

"Cookie!" Jack announced. "I'm going over the side."

Cookie's eyebrow dropped, but his eyes kept smiling.

"Oh, you are, are you?" Cookie said, his eyebrow scrunched. "Jumping ship in midvoyage?"

Cookie rubbed his chin, to consider, and wiped more flour on it. He shrugged. He said, "Ah, Jack. I don't like these steamships. But steam is the new thing. And, oh, don't we know it. New, but somehow suddenly old. Look at how *old* the *Pym* looks, already. Lord! It's all rust and grime. All commotion and corrosion. These steamships have no spirit, my lad. At least, sailing ships take their spirit from the wind!"

Cookie clapped his hands. The flour puffed out in a cloud. Cookie coughed. He said, "But well enough."

Cookie touched Jack's shoulder. He said, "Yes. Well, we've both got to get off her, Jack. But we cannot get off her, just—"

Jack interrupted. "Oh, we can!" he said. "I've got a new plan. We could take that old lifeb—"

"Avast!" Cookie said. "Belay that bad notion." Cookie held up his white hand. "We cannot do it, Jack, because we are *crew*. We are crew, Jack. We signed on, with our own names."

"But—*oh!*" Jack said.

Cookie shook his head. He looked around, and found his pipe. He touched a match against the stove, and it flared.

"Jack, you know that once a man takes a false heading, he cannot always steer himself back to true."

"I can!" Jack said. "I mean—I think I could."

Cookie stuck the long stem of his pipe into his mouth. He held the match to it, and sucked, until he got its tobacco bowl to glowing. Then he puffed out a perfect blue ring of rolling smoke.

"Ah, *hmmm*," Cookie said, watching the smoke ring.

Cookie then blew a smaller smoke ring, right through the first one. And then he blew a third, even smaller ring, through the first two.

Then Cookie reached his hand carefully through all three of the smoky rings and made his hand into a fist. When he pulled his fist back out, it caused the two smaller rings to go inside the first ring. Now the two smaller smoke rings were swirling inside of the big one, creating the swirling bull's-eye of smoke, like a target.

"Make sure of your target," Cookie told Jack.

Jack watched the bull's-eye of smoke, waiting for Cookie to do something to it. Maybe he would make a smoke arrow? Or blow smoke bullets through the ring?

But Cookie just puffed on his pipe. It went *puh, puh, puhp*. Jack and Cookie watched the bull's-eye until it faded and was gone.

"Your target is gone, Cookie," Jack said.

"That's because it's smoke," Cookie said. "I'm an old man. You're a boy. Your target needs be real. What do you want to shoot for, Jack?"

"My target?" Jack said. "It's Moxie. Moxie's island. I've got to get back to Moxie and the sheep dogs."

"And you will," Cookie said. "In time, you will."

"I mean, *now*," Jack said. "Dogs don't live forever. I won't be a boy, forever."

"Sometimes, Jack, I think that you think you might," Cookie said. "But Moxie's there for you, Jack. She'll wait for you, son. She is your good and loyal dog, for always and forever. And remember, a good sailor is forever—"

"No! I'm not a sailor, Cookie. I'm a—I'm a—"

Jack couldn't help himself. He barked.

"Oh, that's funny," said Cookie, not laughing.

"I am worried, Cookie," Jack said. "Things change. Things happen. Sometimes, *bad* things happen. How do I know Moxie's all right? And there are so many islands. How will I know which one?"

"We'll figure it out, when we're back with Captain Day," Cookie assured him. "He can find any island afloat. But now you and I have got to start baking."

Cookie turned and looked down at his breadboard.

"By Jove!" he sputtered. "What is this?"

Jack peered over Cookie's shoulder. Pattered across the breadboard, there was a line of small footprints through the white flour.

"What is it?" asked Jack. "A rat?"

Cookie studied the prints. "Nay," he said. "It's a cat."

"I haven't see a cat."

Cookie chuckled. "And what decent ship's cat would stay on the *Pym*?"

"Maybe it's not a decent cat," Jack said.

They followed the prints, off the breadboard and along the galley counter. The prints were dark where they went through the flour. They became white along the countertop. Near the counter's end, they faded out.

"Where'd it go?" asked Jack. He looked all around.

"Where, indeed?" Cookie said. He swept his pipe stem in an arc around the room. Then he aimed it straight at the flour barrel.

The barrel's lid was halfway off.

"In there," Cookie said.

"In the barrel?" asked Jack.

Cookie chuckled. He walked over to the barrel and looked inside.

"Egad," the old man said.

He took a long wooden spoon and stuck it deep into the flour barrel. With some effort, he lifted it up and out. Hanging limp from the end of the spoon was a furry, floury *thing*.

"It's—an animal," Jack said, stepping back. "And it's dead!"

Cookie grimaced. "Or playing possum," he said.

The thing dropped off Cookie's spoon, back into the barrel.

Both Jack and Cookie leaned close, to peer into it.

Then—*POFF!*

Flour exploded out of the barrel. The lid flipped into the air.

Jack and Cookie jumped back.

The barrel lid went clattering across the floor.

"*Phhhhhhhtttttt!*" came a hiss from the depths of the barrel.

Jack and Cookie looked at each other. Then both of them crept up to the barrel and looked inside.

Jack saw two round yellow eyes with thin black pupils, glaring straight up at him.

He and Cookie looked at each other again.

"Why, the devil—!" Cookie began.

Then—*"Rrrrowrrr!"*

A wild creature burst straight up out of the flour barrel. It fell straight back inside. Then it burst up, again.

Then with another blast, it leaped onto the counter.

"Rrrrowrrr!"

The creature arched its white back and glared at Jack.

"Phhhhht!"

Flour sprayed out of its mouth, as if it was spitting smoke.

Then, *"Rrrrowrrr! Ffffssst!"*

The creature caromed around the galley so fast that it was running on the walls.

It blasted through the cupboards. It knocked over bowls and cups. It sent platters spinning. It sped around the galley. And then, suddenly, it stopped.

A white tornado of flour swirled above it in the air, and then it slowly subsided.

"Hsssssttttt!" The creature glared at Jack with its yellow, marblelike eyes. It *was* a cat.

It was a white cat. Or no—it was a black cat, covered in flour. Its fur was shagged, all different lengths. It looked as if it had jumped through an electric fan. Or as if it had just lost a sword fight with a barber. The cat hissed, crazy and wild. It was fierce, fearsome, and wicked.

Then—*froom!* More flour flew. The cat was off again. It dashed across the room, into a tall closet.

The flour cloud settled.

Then as Jack and Cookie watched, something even stranger happened.

The closet door pulled itself closed.

"The devil!" Cookie said.

Cookie started for the closet. But he paused.

He stepped back. He shook his head. Then he nodded.

He tapped tobacco out of his pipe, and pointed it at the cupboard. "I have half a wise notion to nail that door shut."

Cookie chuckled. "Don't you know, Jack. I read an Edgar Allan Poe story once, about a black cat, which got itself—"

"But, whoa!" Jack interrupted. "Whoa. I mean— what? Did you see all that, Cookie? It stopped my heart. That cat—and then—" Jack motioned toward the closet, his eyes wide.

Cookie chuckled again. He reached inside the pantry to get a match from a tin that was nailed to the wall. He touched the match head to the hot door. The match flared with flame, reminding Jack how hot it was in the galley. Jack wiped his face. He and Cookie were sweating.

"Whew—" Jack whispered. He watched the closet door, and waited for Cookie's next move.

Cookie held the match to his pipe and drew down the flame. He puffed at the pipe stem, and got his tobacco going.

"*Mmm-mfff,*" he puffed. "*Puh, puh, puhp.* All right, then. Let's see. What we have here. A cat in a closet? And who else?"

Cookie pointed down at the deck. There, in the flour spread on the floor, were more new footprints. They led straight into the closet.

And these footprints were different. They were a man's.

"Someone—!" Jack started.

Then his breath caught. He whispered, to Cookie, "Those prints weren't here when I came in."

"Aye." Cookie was nodding. "Aye. Someone has followed you in!"

Cookie stepped to the tall cupboard and yanked open the door.

Then he stepped back, startled.

First, Jack saw the cat.

"*Hhhh-ssssttt!*" it hissed.

"My stars!" Cookie said, to someone. "*Who* are *you*?"

But Jack was looking at the cat. Its arching back had shaggy black fur, gone all snowy with Cookie's best flour. Its yellow eyes had narrow black pupils. Its ragged ears were laid straight back. Its open mouth showed needle teeth, stabbing up and down.

Then Jack noticed what the cat was perched on.

Jack jumped again.

The black cat was on the shoulder of a tall, dark man.

The man was looking over Cookie's shoulder, straight at Jack.

"Who—?" Jack started.

"Who?" the man asked, looking at Jack, not Cookie.

"Who?" the man asked Jack again, when no one answered.

The man waited. Slowly, one black eyebrow raised to his question.

Jack shifted his feet. Was he supposed to answer? He shook his head. He did not know.

The man lowered the eyebrow, and raised the other one. Jack noticed the man's eyes did not match each other. One was large. One was—odd.

The man grabbed his coat's lapel. "Who?" he said. "I am Blackburn Jukes." He tipped his head back. He looked down along his long, straight nose. He stroked his black goatee.

Cookie was not impressed. *"Pffaw!"* he huffed.

But Jack was entranced. What a figure this man cut. His thick black hair was combed back in the older style. His black, narrow eyebrows spread wide and expressive. They shifted and angled as his strange eyes held Jack's.

The man reminded Jack of a famous stage actor. Jack remembered a drawing he had once seen. It was one of that actor who had shot Abraham Lincoln in the theater's balcony. The actor had then jumped down from the balcony and onto the stage. He had broken his leg, but had gotten away.

John Wilkes Booth! thought Jack suddenly. But no, that was long ago. And hadn't John Wilkes Booth been shot and killed by soldiers?

Jukes was smiling at Jack. His white teeth were straight and long. He smiled with his mouth and eyebrows, but not with his eyes. Jack could not help but stare at his eyes. Jukes's left eye was golden brown, large and hypnotic. But his right eye looked off. It was partly closed and lazy. It did not move when the left eye moved, although it radiated a dim and glassy glint. As Jack took all this in, his ears picked up a low buzzing hum. He stuck his fingers into his ears, trying to clear them.

The humming stopped. "Blackburn Jukes," Jukes said, "enters our story."

Wait a minute! Jack thought. *Blackburn Jukes?* Wasn't that the name that the blind digger had spoken? The man for whom the blind man said he worked?

"He's the diggers' boss!" Jack whispered, to Cookie.

And before Jack could consider this further, Jukes stepped from the closet, as if he were stepping onstage.

The cat on his shoulder hissed.

"*Shhhh*, Scorch," Jukes shushed.

The cat hissed again. Neither Jukes nor his cat paid any mind to Cookie.

"*Hssss!*" continued the cat.

"*Ssshhh*, Scorch. *Ssshhhh*."

The cat settled down, with a low, throaty growl.

Jukes brushed flour from his chest. He sighed.

"At last," he said, to Jack, as though they already knew each other.

Jukes regarded Jack, then nodded, satisfied. He said, "I could use a boy like you. Use you. You look like you could dig."

"Oh, balderdash," said Cookie.

But Jack had to ask, "Dig for what? Where?"

"For kauri amber!" said Jukes. "For electrical gold. For bog gum, to make me rich."

"Bog'um?" Jack said.

Jukes chuckled. "Bog gum," he said, again. "Amber."

As he spoke, Jukes's right eye began to glow. An amber light shone from it. It changed to yellow. Then to green. Then back to amber.

Jack glanced at Cookie. Had Cookie seen that?

"Balder and dash!" Cookie sputtered. "Bog gum is a bust. This amber madness will bankrupt New Zealand."

Blackburn Jukes kept smiling at Jack. He never looked at Cookie.

He said, "Not my amber. I have found the mother bog. It has amber, older than petrified. It is electrified. It has soaked up the charges from the earth itself."

"Bog gum!" Cookie mocked him.

"Electric gold!" Jukes said, to Jack.

And what a fine fellow, Jukes seemed. He radiated confidence. Jukes now reached into his watch pocket and pulled out an object about the size of a pocket watch. It was golden, but it wasn't metal. It was round and

smoothed, like a river pebble. And it was almost trans-
parent. It glowed. Jukes tapped it against his white front
teeth. It made a dull *clack*.

"My amber," Jukes said. "Watch this."

He rubbed the amber against his coat sleeve. As he
rubbed, Jack began to hear the low humming again.
What was that? Did it come from the amber, or from
Blackburn Jukes? Jack glanced at Cookie. The old man
heard nothing. Was he too old?

As Jukes rubbed, the amber in his hand had begun
to glow.

"What the—?" Cookie began.

Jukes finished his rubbing with a flurry. He held out
the little object, on his right palm. Light glowed from
inside it.

"Whoa!" said Jack.

The amber glowed in Jukes's hand, but the buzz
sounded in Jack's head. Jack clapped his hands over his
ears. The buzzing continued, the same.

Jukes noticed this, and nodded. He held the amber
up, beside his right eye. The amber and the eye glowed
together. They changed colors together. The buzzing in-
creased.

Then Jukes closed his hand.

"This is good," he said, to Jack. "You are young enough to really hear it."

Jukes snapped his left hand's fingers. Then, like a magician, he reopened his left hand. The amber was gone. The humming had stopped.

"Whoa," said Jack. "Where do you dig it?"

"On my island," said Jukes.

"Your island?" asked Jack.

Then Jukes said something that captured Jack's mind.

"Yes. My island," he said. "With all of its dogs."

"Dogs! Sheep dogs?" asked Jack.

Jukes nodded. "Perhaps, Moxie—"

"*Moxie!*" Jack shouted. "Dog Island!"

Jukes looked down at his fingernails. "As you wish," he said.

Cookie protested. "Now, wait one darned minute—"

But Jack asked, again, "Moxie?

Jukes looked suddenly tired with the conversation. He said, "There is anything we want, if you'll come work for me."

He held out his hand, for Jack to shake.

Jack reached for Jukes's hand. In its palm, he felt the lump of amber. It felt warm and tingling. He heard—and now he felt—the buzzy humming again.

"Moxie?" he asked, again.

Blackburn Jukes nodded.

Then Cookie bumped Jack's hand away.

The humming stopped. The cat hissed.

Jukes noticed Cookie, finally.

He asked, "And you could be—?"

Cookie was growling. "I'm boss o' this galley. And you could be a stowaway."

Jukes discarded Cookie's charge with a flip of his hand.

"The galley boss? That's good," said Jukes. "Because my friend—my cat Scorch—and I are hungry."

"And you'll stay hungry," Cookie told him. "But when Cap'n Gully throws you overboard, you will not be thirsty—"

"Cookie!" Jack chided. He said, to Jukes, again, "Moxie?"

Blackburn Jukes smiled. He raised his thin black eyebrows, and laughed a little laugh of sly amusement. Then he grabbed both his coat's lapels and cleared his throat.

He began practicing his voice, by laughing. It started thin, but became deep and full.

"Ha-ha-hah. Ha-ha-hah. Ha-ha. Ha-hah-*hah*!"

His voice took control of the air in the room. It was

so impressive that it was contagious. Jack began to laugh, too, in almost the same way.

"Ha-hah-*hah*!" came the laugh out of Jack's mouth. "Ha-hah-*hah*!"

Jack enjoyed it, hearing himself. He felt like he was barking.

"Ha-hah-*hah*!"

Cookie glared at Jack. "What in the tarnation—?"

Jack stopped laughing. He grinned and shrugged his shoulders.

Then they all heard Cap'n Gully's roar. And Blackburn Jukes vanished through the hatch.

13

As the afternoon passed, Moxie wondered what old Sage had meant.

Moxie, you must search, Sage's vision had said. *You must look where you haven't looked. You must find what you have never seen.*

Moxie looked down across the high meadow, toward the forest. She realized that she had never explored those dark woods. Whenever she had gone into the woods, she had moved through them quickly, because of the danger from the fangos. Even when Jack had been there before, they never explored the island in its dangerous whole.

Now that the fangos had stopped attacking the sheep,

perhaps the woods would be safer. Moxie could explore them. And who knew? She might find food for the sheep dogs. She might find out something new, about Jack.

But it was now late in the day. Moxie resolved to set out in the morning, to find what she had never seen.

14

Jack!" Cookie shouted.

But Jack dashed out of the galley, chasing after Blackburn Jukes.

Jack ran along the decks, but the day's light was dimming. At first Jack could not find the mysterious man, Jukes. Then he spotted him. He was far aft, in the old lifeboat.

Jukes had climbed into the boat and rolled up its tarpaulin. In the low evening light, he was now busy at the davits. Jukes worked at the ropes, trying to lower the boat into the water. But he couldn't work both ropes at once. So he was letting down the boat, first at one end, and then at the other. A skinny cheroot cigar danced in his teeth.

"Ahoy, there!" Jukes said, when he saw Jack come up to him. Jukes stopped his rope work. He studied Jack with his left eye.

"You can't go," he said, suddenly.

"I can't go?"

Jukes waved a hand toward the horizon. "You cannot go."

"But I don't think—" started Jack.

"Then don't think," interrupted Jukes. "Thinking won't work, with me."

"But I don't—"

"Quiet!" Jukes stopped Jack again. "I have no time for the negative."

Jack was totally confused. "I can't go?"

Had Jack wanted to go? He wasn't sure, now.

Jukes shook his head. "Now wish me luck."

Jukes looked at Jack with a regard almost kindly.

He said. "Well, here. Shake my hand. Man and man."

Jack looked at the lifeboat, and he looked at Jukes. Jukes's great left eye caught Jack's eyes and held them. Jack heard the humming again. It was strange, how the humming did it, but somehow the humming made Jack's thinking slow.

Jack extended his hand for Jukes.

The two shook hands. The humming stopped. It was an eerie, solemn moment.

Then Jukes lifted Jack, by his right arm, straight up off the *Pym*'s deck.

They were nose to nose. "I should have said 'man and boy,'" Jukes said to Jack.

And he flung Jack into the lifeboat.

Jack fell against the rowing bench, making it crack.

Jukes watched Jack a moment, but not to see if he was all right. It was more to see if Jack was capable.

"Take this rope," Jukes said. He swung Jack the rope to the lifeboat's aft davit.

"Now we'll let us down," Jukes said, "when I say, 'Now.'"

Immediately, he ordered, "Now!" Jukes let out his bow rope.

But Jack did nothing, and the lifeboat's bow dipped dangerously.

"Let yours out!" Jukes commanded. "Or we will be dumped."

Jukes fixed Jack with his left eye. Jack let out his rope. The lifeboat lowered onto the water with a jerk and a splash.

"Now let yours go," Jukes ordered.

Jack did. Jukes let go of his rope. The lifeboat floated free from the *Pym*.

It took several long seconds before the stern of the *Pym* passed them. It set the lifeboat to slowly spinning.

Soon, the kauri raft was pulling past the lifeboat. In the gathering evening, Jack saw the diggers on the raft all gathered around their cook fire. The firelight set their sunburned faces aglow. They were smiling.

Jukes called to them. "Ahoy!" The diggers turned to look.

"Ahoy, there!" Jukes called. "Toss a line! Pull us to!"

Two of the diggers stood, to see the lifeboat better. They spoke to the others. But no one moved from the fire.

Jukes swore, now. "Damn it, boys! Come over! Come, toss a line!"

"Good riddance!" shouted one digger.

"At last!" shouted another.

But the diggers did nothing. The raft pulled away from the lifeboat.

Jack's mind suddenly cleared. "Ahoy!" he shouted, but his voice cracked and broke.

Jack thought he heard the little blind man shout something back. But all he could make out was, ". . . the bog gum, Jack!"

The raft pulled away. Its wake set the lifeboat to spinning again. Jukes was standing, and he stumbled as he tried to keep facing the kauri raft.

"You curs!" he shouted at the diggers. "After all I have done!"

But the two diggers who had spoken returned to their cook fire. The *Pym* pulled their raft away, into the dark.

The lifeboat continued to spin. Jukes stumbled as he tried to keep facing the raft.

Finally he muttered, "Of all the ungrateful—!" He sat. He started patting his coat pockets. After some moments, he was able to strike a match.

He lit his cheroot. He pursed his lips. He blew out the smoke, straight at Jack. He picked tobacco off his tongue. He flipped the tobacco at Jack. Then he tipped his head side to side, and considered the sky.

"Mars is close," he said, idly.

Then he pointed at Jack.

"You," he said. "You start to rowing."

15

After listening to the visions of Kelso and Sage, Moxie ran straight to the sheep. She barked, to get the attention of the sheep dogs on guard. She gave them brave Kelso's noble command.

"Be vigilant!" she told Boffo.

"Be vigilant!" she told Cam.

But all the sheep dogs merely watched her, without any interest.

"We must be vigilant," Moxie told them, "because we are dogs!"

But as she looked at her starving friends, Moxie realized they were looking less like dogs every day. They were skinny. Their ribs showed. They were mangy. Their lower eyelids drooped.

Moxie said it again, but weakly, this time. "We are dogs—"

Suddenly, she had trouble believing it, herself.

"I am going in the morning, into the woods. Maybe I'll find something for us."

But the dogs had all turned away from her. They were looking down toward the woods, already.

Moxie turned, too, and she saw them.

Fangos.

They were there, slinking among the trees at the edge of the meadow.

"Stay here!" Moxie said to the sheep dogs guarding the sheep. She headed down through the meadow toward the trees and the fangos. She held her head up, and raised her hackles. She lay back her ears, and curled her upper lip. She was going to show everyone how a true dog acted.

But as she neared the first line of trees, Moxie felt herself slow. Her head dropped. Her eyes darted, back and forth. Inside her chest, her heart began to pound faster and faster. And faster.

Strangely, her heart also pounded weaker and weaker. Her legs began to quiver. Her knees began to shake.

What she felt she must do and what she was actually doing were two different things.

Moxie stopped before she got to the edge of trees. The fangos were in there. She smelled their rank bodies. But she couldn't see them.

Then she did see them.

Then she didn't.

The fangos drifted in and out through the trees. It was like they were there, and they were not there, too. They were visible. They were invisible. They seemed half imaginary.

The dire fangos had once been good sheep dogs themselves. But they had given up their dogness and had become wild things. Maybe that was why they were half invisible. Maybe fangos were only half there. Without dog souls, they were fangos. They were empty shells.

As Moxie had these thoughts, the fangos appeared closer, almost as if they had been called by her mind. They appeared in the darkness between the nearest trees. They were like shadows that had come alive.

Terrified, Moxie snarled, and the fangos disappeared.

16

Hours later, lightning was flashing. In the small boat on the open sea, Jack had rowed until his arms burned and ached.

Facing Jack, Blackburn Jukes loafed in the stern of the lifeboat, smoking another little cheroot cigar. Every time Jukes puffed, his right eye glowed red.

Sometimes, Jukes hummed. He hummed tunes and ditties. Sometimes, Jukes hummed the low buzz Jack had heard on the *Pym*. This buzzing got inside Jack's head, and fogged his brain. Jack had to shake his head, to resist it. He felt that if he let it, it would take over his mind.

Twice, Jack asked Jukes about dogs on the island. The

first time, Jukes said nothing. The second time, Jukes spat. He said, "Dogs? What dogs?"

Jukes shrugged. He puffed. His eye pulsed red, with his cheroot.

"A storm is brewing," Jukes said, now, coolly.

Jukes had his left arm around a round black hatbox, which looked to be made out of patent leather. He kept his other arm wrapped around the boat's steering tiller.

Jukes leaned to the tiller. "Pull harder," he ordered.

Jack faked pulling harder.

Puff. Puff. Juke's right eye pulsed with his cigar. "Pull!" he ordered.

Jack tried to pull, but he had lost much of his strength, and the lifeboat was getting harder to move. Just as Jack had predicted, the lifeboat was leaking. Water now sloshed over the tops of Jack's toes.

Blackburn Jukes noticed this. He stood and peered over Jack's shoulders, into the direction in which they were heading. *Puff. Puff.* He flicked his cheroot up into the air. It fell into the sea, like a shooting star.

"Well, well. At least we are getting there," he said.

Jack turned to look, but Jukes ordered, "Bail!"

Jukes tossed a canvas bailing bag to Jack. "All of the water. Out of the boat," he commanded.

Jack was happy to change jobs, to get to use different muscles. And bailing made more sense now. It would help to keep the lifeboat afloat.

Jack was also able to turn around as he worked. He strained to see where they were going. At first, that appeared to be a flat black nowhere. It was like they were heading into a big blank curtain.

But then lightning flashed, revealing a low cloud. Lightning flashed again. A big dark shape loomed beneath the cloud. Jack peered. Lightning flashed. It was an island! It was near, almost at hand. The black island rose, massive, dense, and steep.

Jukes liked what he saw. He lit another cheroot. "Hah! Boy! Bail!" he commanded.

Jack got down on his knees. He began to scoop water out of the lifeboat and into the sea. But the bailing bag was heavy. Within minutes, Jack was aching more from the bailing than he had ached from the hours of rowing.

To lighten his load, Jack scooped less water with every bag. But new water kept leaking into the lifeboat. As the water got deeper, the boat leaked faster.

"Curse it!" Jukes shouted. "Stop bailing and row!"

Jack dropped the bailing bag and sat on the bench. He tried to row.

"No! Bail!" Jukes commanded.

Lightning flashed again. There was the island, hard ashoulder.

"Bail! Row! Bail!" Jukes shouted.

Jack rowed, and bailed, but he was too tired. It now felt to Jack that the boat was not even moving. It was foundering in place, and sinking.

"Row, damn it!" Jukes thundered. "Bail, damn it. Bail!"

Jack tried. He couldn't. He lifted the bailing bag, but he could not get it over the side. The water poured back inside the boat.

"*Arghh*—" Jukes stood. He towered over Jack.

Jack flinched, expecting a beating.

Instead, Jukes ordered, "Quiet!"

Jack didn't speak. Jukes whispered, "*Shhh*. Ship the oars! Belay that bailing!" Jukes set the hatbox down next to Jack. It fell off the bench, into the water.

Jack rested, his back bent. He was trying to listen. He thought he heard a faint, hushlike hissing, but he was too tired to imagine its source.

Jack's neck muscles cramped. Water sloshed around his calves. Jukes's hatbox floated against Jack's leg.

"There! Listen!" Jukes said.

Jack tried to listen. There was a hissing.

Then Jukes began to laugh.

"Ha-HAH! Ha-HAH! Look!" Jukes gloated. "Ha-HAH! Hear that? We are here!"

Jack could not lift his eyes. He was watching the hatbox. It was tumbling in the boat water. It seemed to be moving under its own power.

Or was Jack just getting dizzy? The hissing was getting louder. It was becoming a white roar.

Weary, Jack looked in the direction of the roar. He saw that the black cloud had quit with its lightning. The sky was breaking up, letting through shafts of silver moonlight.

The lifeboat sat dead in the water. Ten thousand moons were reflected in the chop of the sea.

The moonlight glinted off Blackburn Jukes's white teeth. He kept laughing and laughing. "Ha-hah! Ha-ha-HAH! Ha-ha-ha-ha-HAH!" He was pointing.

Jack looked again toward the land. He saw a dim break in the lumpy black wall of the island. It was a narrow, vertical opening, barely wide enough for a ship.

"Ha-HAH! There!" Jukes laughed, jabbing his finger

toward the opening. "Ha-HAH! Ha-ha-HAH! We are here."

Juke's laughter was loud, but the roaring was growing louder. Jack now saw a bouncing line of white in the water, nearer to the lifeboat than to the land.

It was surf, breaking near shore. From the boat, it appeared as a dancing white froth.

"Uh-oh," Jack said. He pointed at the froth.

Then Jack felt a swell lift the boat and move it closer to the surf. The lifeboat was so full of water that it was barely afloat.

"Uh-oh," Jack said, loudly, for Jukes to hear.

Jukes looked down at Jack.

"You'll be my digger," he said, quite cheerfully. "Report for duty, tomorrow."

Jack said, "What—?"

But his words were swallowed by the roar. Another swell lifted the lifeboat closer to the breakers.

The boat lifted again, right up to the surf's crest.

"Ha-HAH!" Blackburn Jukes laughed. "Ha-HAH! Ha-HAH!"

Then in the way many things happen, suddenly but slowly, the lifeboat turned once and pitched over the top of the surf's crest. Jack looked around for something to grab, and the boat slid down the steep face of a wave.

FWOOMPSH!

At the wave's bottom, the boat tipped backward and swamped.

FWUSH!

It filled with dark water.

SHWUSH!

Jack and everything washed out of the boat.

Brrrrrrng! Jack's ears filled with foam. *Hsssh!* Then he was under—without sound, in the darkness. Nothing to see. Nothing to breathe. Jack windmilled his arms and bicycled his legs in the black water.

He bumped against something. Or someone. Was it Jukes? Jack grabbed whoever it was, and tried to climb up it, to the surface.

But it kicked him, square in the stomach.

Ka-huh!

The kick knocked all of Jack's air out of his mouth in one silver shimmering explosion of bubbles.

Huhh! Jack thrashed and flailed, reaching for anything. Was he sinking? Rising? Drowning? Dying?

Strangely, Jack remembered he had been through a near drowning before. That time—*When was it?*—he had survived. This time? Who knew? Would this be the end?

But Jack's fingers brushed something. He grabbed it. It was round. It was buoyant. He held on to the thing with both hands, and pulled it to his chest. His face broke through to air. He gulped a big lungful. Jack clung to the thing, hard. It supported him. He floated. Then he realized he was inside the line of surf.

Here, the water was calmer. Holding on to his float, Jack slowly scissor-kicked, away from the surf. Soon his feet touched bottom. He was able to stand. He swayed. He dropped his lifesaving float, with a splash. Jack staggered toward the shore, pushing the float in front of him. He had made it. Again.

That notion impressed Jack. He thought about who he was—just who—at this moment of survival. He was Jack. JACK. He was Jack, alone, but alive. He felt tired and half drowned, but far from half dead.

Indeed, at this moment, Jack felt almost immortal.

He didn't think the word *immortal*. Actually, *unkillable* was the word that went through Jack's mind.

Unkillable, he thought. *I wonder if I am?*

Jack laughed quietly, both with himself and at himself. He felt like he was his own friend.

He knew he was lucky. "But lucky is good," he said. His wonderful friend Cookie had often said so.

Jack waded, thigh-deep now, toward the beach. He kicked before him the round float. He saw it was the patent-leather hatbox he had seen Jukes holding in the lifeboat. In front of him, the box rolled over by itself in the water.

What was inside it? Jack bent down and examined it under the dim moonlight. The box's lid had a latch. Jack pried it open with his thumb.

"Ffffffffffttttttt!!!!!"

It had fury inside it.

It was Jukes's cat, Scorch. Scorch burst from the hatbox. He clawed in a flash straight to the top of Jack's head.

"Fffft!" Scorch hissed. He claws daggered deep into Jack's scalp.

"Ffffft! Ffffft!"

"Y-y-yah!" Jack yelled. *"Y-y-yah!"*

He beat at the cat on his head. "Hey! Hey!"

"Ffffft!" The cat would not let go. He grappled Jack's head.

In pain, Jack dropped to his knees. He ducked his head underwater. The cat gave him one more claw stab, and let go.

Jack came back up. There was the cat, swimming in the shallow water toward shore. With his tail snaking behind him, Scorch looked like a midget sea monster.

Scorch reached the shore, and jumped out of the water onto the sand. There, he stood, sputtering and hissing. He shook each leg, one at a time. He hopped angrily up to the dry sand.

There, Scorch turned and looked back toward Jack. "*Wrrrrrr—*" he cursed.

Then he disappeared.

Jack dunked his head into the seawater again. He rubbed his scalp. "Oh, *ow. Ow*," he said.

He waded ashore. Where was he? It became darker. The cloud had covered the moon. The island's steep cliffs were a blank, black wall. Behind Jack, the line of surf kept roaring and hissing. Jack peered up and down the beach. He saw no sign of Jukes. Had he drowned?

This time, the thought of someone drowning made Jack feel mortal and weak. His knees buckled. He sank to the sand.

He fell asleep, sitting up.

Moxie was awake at dawn, getting ready to go explore the woods. She had spent much of the night watching the moon. It had passed behind clouds as the lightning flashed. Electricity had lifted her fur and dropped it, again and again. She had howled at the moon, to announce her intentions. Once, a bolt of lightning blasted the top of the sea cliffs.

Moxie wanted the sheep dogs to know she was going.

"I'm off," she told Mother Molly and her puppies.

"Good luck. Be careful," Molly said.

"I'll be back," she told Cam and Boffo, and the other herders.

They looked at her, but said nothing.

Moxie went to the highest cliff top, but Blur wasn't

there. She saw him, far away, along the lower cliffs, waiting for the seabirds.

Moxie padded past the old rock wall. This was where the lightning had struck, and the ground was blasted up. There, at the wall, something stopped her. It was a scent. It was strong. In the shallow hole left by the lightning, Moxie sniffed at the scent, which was mixed with the buzzy odor of the lightning's electricity.

The scent was of old Sage. As Moxie sniffed, Sage's vision appeared in front of her.

Moxie, Sage's vision said to her. *I have wonderful news. What you seek to find is beyond the woods, near a cove of the ocean. Go, now. Go now—*

And Sage's vision faded.

Moxie scratched the ground and sniffed at it again. She couldn't find more scent, but she felt charged by Sage's words. She trotted down through the meadow. She passed through the old apple orchard where she and Jack had once faced the fangos. From there, she trotted through the deeper forest and through a clearing where the fangos had once tried to eat her. But she saw no fangos, this time. It was a good feeling. She remembered Sage's words. She asked herself, *What do I seek to find?*

She could only answer, *Jack!*

Jack had slept the night, sitting on the beach. He slept without moving and without having dreams.

He awoke cross-legged, with his chin on his chest. He stayed still for a moment, listening to the surf behind him. It was a roar and a hiss, a foamy static.

Jack didn't lift his head, for a while. He studied the sand between his legs. He remembered that he had woken on a beach like this once before. It seemed long, long ago, when he had been cast away by his shipmates. Then, he had washed up on Moxie's island. Jack wished he were there again. In a way, he wished it were one year before.

But he was here now. It was a bright, hot, island morning. What island was this? Jack had no idea.

Jack's shirt had mostly dried. It stuck to his back. His trouser knees were caked with dry sand. The sand trickled out of the creases, like time falling through an hourglass. Jack put his hand under his knee to catch some of the grains. He threw them over his shoulder for good luck.

Jack cleared his throat. Hearing the sound of it made him feel that he should say something about this occasion. But he couldn't think of any words.

So he lifted his head. In front of him in the sand, the footprints of Jukes's cat, Scorch, tracked away, up the beach. Tenderly, Jack felt the cat's scratches in his scalp. They had scabbed over, and now they itched.

"Blast that blasted cat," he said, aloud.

Then he looked around him, for Blackburn Jukes.

No Jukes.

Well, there, Jack thought. He had said something, at least, even though it was a curse. But as Cookie sometimes said, cursing sometimes works.

To his own ears, on the beach, Jack's voice had sounded distant and echoey. He still had water in his ears. He shook his head, to get it out. Then he stood. He stretched.

"Well, now!" he said, to himself. "Look around."

This wasn't even a bona fide beach. It was barely a low strand, a mere fifty yards deep. It arced out away from the island's tall cliffs, going from Jack's left to his right.

Between the narrow strand and the cliffs was a calm, pretty channel of clear green water. Where the strand connected to the island, the channel bent and passed behind the cliffs, through the opening that Jack and Jukes had seen, the night before.

Even as close as Jack was to it, it was hard to make out the opening, because the cliffs on each side of it were covered with the same gray-green scrub. Jack walked along the strand toward the opening, kicking sand over the tracks of the cat. When he got to the opening, he could not see much from there, either. The channel bent back hard to the right as it passed behind the cliff. The opening was like a hidden, secret passage.

Jack stuck out his lower lip and raised his eyebrows. He was beginning to like this, as mysterious as it was. The cliffs on both sides of the opening were nearly sheer. Their brush was impenetrable, as thick as a donkey's coat. The tracks of the cat led into the brush, but Jack had no way off this strand, except by swimming in the channel, through this mysterious passage.

And why not? Jack thought. It was just like in books.

So Jack waded into the channel's water, and found it cooler than the ocean. It felt fresher, too. Jack tasted it. It was briny, but not as salty as the sea. The channel quickly deepened, and Jack began to swim, up the middle of the channel.

He swam slowly into the opening, breaststroking to keep his head up. After the channel passed through the cliffs, it veered back to the left. There, it opened into a cove.

The cove was like a picture. It was beautiful, and as round as a teacup. It was about the size of the Old Rec ballpark, back in San Francisco before the earthquake. The cove's water was clear green, too, although not as dark as the channel's.

And its surface was smooth, except—

Jack stopped swimming, and treaded water. The cove's smooth surface was punctured by poles. But they were more than mere poles. They were the tops of masts of ships that had sailed into the cove and had sunk. Jack counted seven masts, leaning at angles. They appeared to belong to three different ships, perhaps two sloops and a schooner. The masts were grayed with age, but from two of them there still hung some rotten canvas and riggings. One mast still had one yard, hanging at a cant.

These ships had somehow sunk here. Or they had been scuttled. A long time ago? Or when?

Jack wanted to pause longer, but he was tiring. So he swam quietly between the masts. Beyond them curved the cove's white crescent beach. Behind the beach grew green brush, and behind the brush grew trees.

But these weren't just any trees.

They were giant kauris, like the logs that were towed behind the steamer *Pym*. And these were the largest kauris that Jack had ever seen. He had heard that a few giants still remained in New Zealand. Now he knew he must be seeing them.

These kauris grew twelve stories tall, and more. They were so stout that their trunks appeared to be swollen. The trunks were ten feet thick. The trees were giants. They were so big they were grotesque, and they made this pretty little teacup of a cove appear to shrink into a smaller dimension.

It all made Jack feel as if he himself were growing smaller as he swam toward the great trees and stepped out of the water. What a feeling! It was spooky, but strangely thrilling.

Jack looked around at the cove with its ghostly ship masts. He was now out of sight of the ocean, out of sound of the surf. The cove lay in an almost perfectly round, steep-sided basin. But inland, behind the giant kauri trees, the hillsides appeared to be less steep. Jack could not see a path from where he was, but he thought he saw a narrow gap, which might be an exit. Jack felt an impulse to head straight for the gap. But he looked again at the giant kauris, and felt he had to explore them.

Jack scouted around, looking up into the high crowns. The sun shone down through their branches. Birds flew past their trunks. On the ground, the trees' shade was patchy. Jack stumbled over a root. He recovered. He tripped again, and he fell.

He hit the ground with a hollow *thump*. He got up on his knees, and looked around himself.

Jack had tripped over a door. He stood and looked down at it. It was a wooden door, leading into the earth itself. The door wasn't flat on the ground. It lay at a low angle. It was not a perfect rectangle. It had been carved into an odd shape, to fit between the giant roots.

What now? Jack wondered. *Some kind of a cellar?*

The door was almost hidden by branches fallen from above. Jack swept away the litter, and found the door's handle. It was a thick leather strap, aged but sturdy. Jack found a long tree limb and used it as a lever to pry the door up. He propped the door open with another stout limb.

A dank, spongy odor rose immediately from the opening. Jack recoiled, but sunlight shone down into the doorway and made its interior visible.

"Whoa!" Jack muttered. He descended a few stair steps. He crouched so that he could peer farther back into the cellar.

It was a huge, rounded chamber, dank and earthy. Roots hung from its ceiling. But there were things inside it. In the light from the doorway, Jack saw two kegs of rum, a barrel of nails, what looked like an open cask of black pepper, and three ship's strongboxes. Two of the strongboxes were locked closed with padlocks. The other box was open. It brimmed with gold coins.

"Treasure!" Jack shouted.

He whispered, "Somebody was rich."

Jack checked behind himself, then went down inside the cellar. Carefully, he began to poke his way around. Against one strongbox leaned a bent bicycle. A cash register sat on the floor, broken open. Farther back, Jack saw stranger sights. There were a suit of knight's armor, a stuffed armadillo, and a stuffed Andean condor with a twelve-foot wingspan. The giant vulture was perched on an Ecuadoran battle flag, which was either bloodied or paint spattered. Next to that, there was a large wicker basket heaped with shattered colors. It looked like it was filled with broken glass lampshades. Farther back still, several large bolts of bright cloth leaned against what appeared to be a large pile of tinned food, mainly roast beef and crackers.

"Well, now," Jack whispered. "Call me Sir Arthur Evans." He was reminded of Sir Arthur's recent discoveries of treasure at Knossos, on Crete.

Jack also found a barrel of salted peanuts.

"Real treasure!" he said. He filled his pockets with them.

Then he saw something else, on a crude table far back in the cellar. The way it dimly glowed with a faint golden light, it almost looked like a Japanese paper lantern with a candle inside it. Jack walked back to it. But it wasn't a lantern of any kind he had seen. It looked like a glowing rock.

Jack picked it up. It was heavy, and almost warm.

"Wait a minute," he said. He knew what it was. It must be a big lump of the amber that Jukes had shown him and Cookie.

"It's bog gum," Jack said.

He set the amber down. He went back and stuck his head up through the doorway. He looked across the kauri grove from ground level.

There! He saw another door. It was so well camouflaged that it was almost invisible. This door was fashioned right into the side of the biggest tree's trunk.

Jack climbed out of the cellar and went to the door. A sign above the door read, **VERBODEN!** in big black letters that looked angry.

It was a foreign word, *verboden*. Jack guessed that it meant "forbidden," or at least, "Keep Out!" That's what angry signs usually meant.

But Jack noticed something else on the sign. Someone had taken a knife and scratched into it—in English, this time—*Dutchman's Cove.*

Dutchman's Cove. Jack nodded, considering the cove and the sunken ships. Cookie had told him stories of the early Dutch explorers.

The door was as upright as the tree it was built into, but its corners were no more squared than the door to the cellar. This door had been designed to fit perfectly within the shapes of the tree bark. It had two brass hinges—off a ship most probably—as well as a solid brass handle with a thumb latch, and a big white knocker.

The knocker was made of ivory, probably from a walrus tusk. Carved into the knocker was the face of a skull. The skull had two big holes for its black eyes, two dots for its nostrils, and two rows of perfectly rectangular teeth. The skull's teeth reminded Jack of Blackburn Jukes's teeth, and his smile.

Jack walked around, behind the huge tree. In the other side of it, there was a high window. It wasn't squared either, but its four glass panes were unbroken. The window had been there for so long that the glass was beginning to warp.

The window was set too high for Jack to look into, so he went back around to the door side of the tree. There, he couldn't help himself. He reached for the knocker below the sign that said **VERBODEN!**

But before he could knock, there was a noise behind him.

Then a voice.

"Verboden!"

Jack turned.

There stood Blackburn Jukes.

Moxie had settled into a steady dogtrot. At this pace, she wouldn't tire, no matter how far it was to Sage's cove. After some time, she came upon an old trail. The trail led her down through a clearing, then into a small valley, then into a narrow ravine.

Moxie trotted along. She felt fully a dog, again. She was going to meet her human.

20

Reporting for duty?" Blackburn Jukes said.

He stood before Jack, with his feet set wide and his hands on his hips. He was smiling his thin smile. He looked like a famous dead actor. One eyebrow cocked up, the other bent down. His right eye was glassy and glinting dully. His left eye bored into Jack's mind.

"*Verboden*," Jukes said. "Can't you read?"

Jack nodded, then he shook his head. He was becoming confused. Then he realized he was hearing a humming.

Jukes clucked his tongue. He looked Jack up and down. He said, "*Hmm*—are you ready to dig?"

Jack looked around, out through the kauri trees. He could make out the far hillside where he had seen the gap that might be a way out.

"Don't even think of it," Jukes said. *"Hmm—?"*

Could Jukes read Jack's mind? Jack looked into Jukes's left eye. The power in it set Jack to blinking. The humming grew. It felt as though it was getting inside Jack's brain.

Jack put his hands over his ears. But the humming became like an electrical buzzing. It buzzed Jack's teeth. It buzzed down his spine. It made the hair on his neck stand up. *What is this?* Jack wondered. Then he understood. This felt like *fear.*

Then the humming stopped. Jukes smiled. He was enjoying this.

"And now," he said. "I want you to—"

Jack bolted.

He dashed away. The feeling of fear had charged him with energy. He dodged behind a great kauri tree. Then he darted behind another. Then he sprinted, all out, toward the hillside.

As he ran, the buzzy fear feeling evaporated. But behind him, Jack heard Jukes's powerful actor's voice booming.

"You'll be back!" Jukes bellowed.

"You'll be back!

"You'll be back! Ha, ha!

"Ha ha ha ha ha ha *hah!*"

21

Moxie was loping now, downhill toward Jack. Hope was pulling her along, by her heart.

22

As his fear disappeared, Jack felt the joy of escape.

Ha, ha, hah! Jack was thinking as he dashed out the back of the kauri grove. *Ha, ha, ha! Ha, ha, ha! Who gets the last ha-ha now?*

He was running toward the nearest hillside, but he splashed to a stop in a marshy bog. The bog appeared to continue, so Jack turned left. He skirted the bog, until he found his way to the far hillside.

Jack headed for the gap through the hills. At first, he ran hard. Then he jogged. Then he walked. He staggered some, and struggled. But Jack kept moving.

Finally, he felt safe. He almost wondered why he had run. Jack laughed. What was he afraid of? He dared to look behind. There was no one there, of course. He was feeling much better. It was wonderful, really, how quickly life changed.

"Ha, ha, ha!" Jack laughed, musically.

He entered a small, wooded valley. Soon, the valley constricted into a ravine. Then the ravine grew more narrow, and became a tight passage.

Here, Jack stopped. Something was odd about this place, too. The passage seemed to be a kind of natural gate. But it felt unnatural, as well. Jack looked up, and studied both its steep sides. There were boulders up there. Could they fall on him? They could. Especially, if pushed by a man.

Jack walked slowly through the defile, always looking up, ready to run or dodge rolling boulders. He soon entered a thick stand of saplings and small trees. Strangely, some of the small trees were leaned over, bent nearly double.

Jack was turning as he walked. He had just enough time to think, *Strange.*

Then, *shwhoosh!*

Like he was kicking a football, Jack's right leg yanked out from under him. He was jerked into the air, upside down. His head banged against the ground, once, twice. Then he was hoisted, bouncing, up into the air.

Jack hung by his right ankle, upside down, bouncing on the end of a rope tied to the top of a young tree.

He had been caught in a snare. Blood rushed into Jack's head. His face swelled. His heart thudded in his ears. Jack moaned against the pressure. He tried to bend at his waist to reach up and untie the rope, but he wasn't strong enough. He hung there, bouncing.

He began to slowly spin, like a fly on a strand of spiderweb. The world spun around him, upside down. Around. And around. He began to get dizzy. He held out his arms, and that slowed his spin.

Jack looked up, or down, from his upside-down position. He saw the rope went from his ankle to the top of a small, bent-over tree. The treetop was swaying and bouncing, back and forth. Jack figured that just maybe, if he could get himself to swinging, he could swing over and grab hold of the little tree's trunk. Then he could shinny up the tree to take the tension off the rope, and get himself out of this trap.

So Jack let his arms drop, toward the ground. Then using them as weights, he slowly began to build a swinging motion, back and forth, back and forth. It took a long time. The little tree was so limber that its bouncing dampened the swinging movements, but finally Jack got going a decent swing. Back. Forth. Swing. Swing.

Jack swung closer and closer to the snare tree's trunk. He reached. He almost grabbed it. He hoped the next swing would do the trick. Jack knew he shouldn't hurry, but on the next swing he tried too hard. At the top of the back swing, Jack gave his body an extra bit of *oomph*.

And, *snap!* That broke the rope.

Jack fell. As he fell, he twisted so he would not hit his head again. He thumped hard, with his whole left side, flat on the ground. His wind knocked out. His whole side stung, then went numb. All his nerves tingled and ached.

Jack lay still, waiting for normal feelings to come back to his side. He expected pain. He got some, but it wasn't too bad. He listened—for whatever might happen to him, next.

He felt beleaguered. But he felt alive.

Here he was. *Here I am,* he thought. Alive. *I am alive again for the second time in two days.*

That sounded almost funny, to think of it like that. Jack tried to laugh, but his ribs hurt. He sat up, and untied the snare loop from around his ankle. The rope was rotten. The snare may have been set and waiting for years.

That made Jack sad. Everything here was so old—Dutchman's Cove, the trees, the doors, the cellar, even the snare. Maybe no one else was on this island but Jack himself and Blackburn Jukes.

Then Jack remembered that he had been alone on an island before, and things had worked out well for him, for a while.

Jack got to his feet. He shook himself out. He scratched his scalp, where the cat had ridden his head to the beach. Then Jack began walking again, carefully and slowly, up through the defile.

23

Moxie was now running as fast as she could. She barely missed several tree trunks as she sped down through a wooded valley.

Then something made her pull up and slow to a stop.

It was a scent.

No, it was two scents, together. And together they confused her.

She sniffed at the scents. One was—

Yes, it was! It was human.

It had to be. It could be Jack's scent, couldn't it be?

Yes, it could be! Except for that second scent, with it. The second scent was different, full of ammonia and strangeness. What was it? Moxie had never smelled anything like it before. It was eccentric and arrogant. It was certainly not a dog.

Moxie started moving again, more slowly than before.

Finally, the two scents had become so strong that she had to stop and sit down.

What is it? she wondered, sniffing the air.

Then something came walking up the path toward her.

And then it stopped.

24

Jack had followed the path as it continued uphill. In spite of his tangle with the snare, he began to daydream about finding Moxie.

The daydream made him sleepy. Soon, Jack stopped walking. He stood still for a moment and put his hands on his hips. He smiled and thought about Moxie. He tried to imagine what she looked like.

At first, it wasn't easy. So he closed his eyes.

Then he opened them.

And there she was.

Jack enjoyed the daydream.

Then his mouth fell open.

Because—*there she was*. She was there, her vision, in front of him. Jack saw a little black-and-white Border collie, sitting in the trail, as still as a picture. There she was. She was there. *Right there.*

Jack blinked.

Moxie's image sat looking at him, her head tilted to one side.

She looked more than surprised. She looked amazed.

Jack tilted his head, too, but in the opposite way from the image's.

Then the little image dog shifted her head's tilt, to match Jack's.

Oh, my, Jack thought. He shut his eyes. He put his hands to his face and kept his eyes shut. He kept the image going in his mind. In his mind, he saw his real Moxie and her beauty, and her loyalty, and her courage. Could he open his eyes, now, and see her, here, for real? Was she here? Was this her? Was this real?

Jack opened his eyes.

And she was gone.

Jack shrugged. He smiled at himself. *But of course,* he thought.

Then he looked down.

There she was. At his feet. Gazing up.

"Moxie!"

Her black-and-white face. Her one eye so blue. Her

other eye brown. Her face full of love. Her intelligence. Loyalty. Jack's Moxie.

"Moxie!" Jack cried. "Moxie! Moxie! Moxie!"

He fell to his knees. He tried to hug her as she licked his face, but she squirmed so much that he couldn't hold her. He started laughing. He laughed and he laughed. He rolled on the ground. *Moxie! Moxie!* He kept trying to hug her. But she was too energetic. She wiggled and squirmed. She shook. She trembled. At last, she settled down.

Jack held her. He felt her ribs. Moxie was gaunt.

She was starving!

"Oh, Moxie!" Jack cried.

"Moxie—!" he started. But what else could he say? "Moxie, you need to eat."

Moxie rolled over onto her back in the dirt of the trail. Jack lay down next to her, and rubbed her chest and belly. She was all bones and hollowness. But she wasn't empty. She was full of happiness, too. Jack started laughing again.

Moxie got back on her feet. She sniffed at Jack's hair. She sniffed and she sniffed. She couldn't get enough of the smell.

But it made her sneeze. She sneezed again, and shook

her head. Then she covered Jack's face with licking kisses.

"Come on, Moxie," Jack said. "Let's go up to the meadow. Let's see what's up, what's going on." He rose and they started walking up the path.

25

Moxie had experienced their reunion in her own way.

When the something had approached her, she was stunned into stillness.

What is this? Moxie sniffed, but the strange mix of scents confused her.

It looked like a human.

But who was this human? Who could it be?

Then it spoke. "Moxie!"

It dropped to its knees. It reached out with its forelegs.

"Moxie! It's you!"

Moxie nearly fainted. She nearly fell over.

It's me! she told him.

"Yes, it's you!"

Yes, it is. It's me. And it's you.

"Yes, it's me! Moxie, how are you?"

I missed you.

"Oh, dog, I missed you!"

And I—but wait? What's that smell on you, Jack?

"Your ribs—Moxie! You're too skinny."

I'm hungry. But I'm happy. But what is that smell?

"Oh, my dog. Oh, my dog."

But, Jack. What's that smell? It's not you. But it's on you. In your hair. Some animal. It's so strange, so—pungent.

Moxie shook her head and sneezed out the odor. Then she covered Jack's face with kisses. She even tried to lick the smell out of his hair.

She told him, *Don't you ever leave me again.*

"I won't leave you, Moxie."

I believe you, Jack, Moxie told him. *You are my boy, Jack. I will always believe you.*

26

As they walked up the trail, Jack could feel Moxie's thoughts. They were saying, *Everything is fine. I could die right now, and I would be a happy sheep dog.*

"Don't you worry," Jack told Moxie. "I am going to find you some food."

Jack thought about the food in the cellar back at the kauri grove. He could sneak back there and bring up some supplies. But, no, Jack didn't want to risk losing what he had just found.

"So come on, Moxie," he said. "We'll work something out. I want to see my old home."

Jack led the way through the woods. Every time he stopped, Moxie bumped into the backs of his legs. This was Moxie's island, but Jack had never seen this part of it. When he had lived on the island, this had all been fango territory. Jack sensed that it lay below the old apple orchard, where he and Moxie had once been surprised by the fangos and surrounded.

That time, Jack had panicked and fled, leaving Moxie to defend herself against the fangos. It wasn't until the great fango battle, on his last day on the island, that Jack had found the courage he needed to fight a good fight.

Remembering his past courage made Jack feel brave now. But thinking about courage reminded Jack of fear. A chill tickled his soul, just as a cold nose of a fango had once touched the back of his neck.

Ah—fangos! Jack thought. He slowed. Moxie passed him. Jack reached down and picked up a big broken tree limb. He held it with two hands and swung it, for practice.

Moxie stopped, and looked back at him. *Why the stick?* she wondered. *That's too big to play fetch.*

Jack didn't understand her. "I'm not afraid," he told her.

Moxie led on. Jack asked himself, *Was I ever really brave? Can I be brave again? Can a person be brave without first being scared?*

Moxie looked back to tell him, *Of course you can,* but Jack was unsure. He wondered what courage was, exactly. It seemed an easy thing to see in others, but hard to feel in oneself.

Jack realized he was having thoughts he had not had for almost a year. Oh, he had had many thoughts in the past year, but those thoughts had all been daydreams and fantasies. Here, on a deserted island, talking with a dog, his brain felt clear and more focused. Jack looked around at the forest. He looked down at his hands. Everything looked more real.

Moxie, padding in front of him, was as real as life could get. Jack smiled. *Dear Moxie,* he thought, *not only am I able to really talk to a dog, but—guess what?—I can really talk with myself, again. I mean, I can think.*

Moxie looked back over her shoulder. *How's that?* she wondered.

Things are good, Jack told her. *Lead on.*

So Moxie led on. Jack used the big limb as a walking stick. It reminded him of the walking staff he had used to fight the fangos. He swung it again, left and right. He would have to find out what had happened to the derelict fangos.

After some time, they arrived at the old apple orchard. They emerged onto the broad, hilltop meadow. To Jack, it looked beautiful. It was green and flower filled, fragrant and warm. It lay beneath a yellow sun in a blue, open sky.

Jack stopped, to let his heart beat. He breathed in huge, swelling breaths.

"Ah!" he breathed. "Ah! Ah!"

Moxie barked at him, once. Then she barked again, in the direction of the top of the meadow. Jack saw the heads of several sheep dogs pop up, over a rise.

"Hey! Friends!" Jack cried. He began to run. He ran up through the meadow, past the spring, beyond his old shelters, and into the high pasture.

Jack didn't know what he had expected, but he was surprised. He saw a dozen dirty, matted sheep huddled on a nearly bare patch of ground.

It was sad to see. But what shocked him more was what he noticed next.

The sheep were guarded by five wretched creatures.

Fangos, Jack thought. But he realized that these weren't fangos.

These were real dogs. They were sheep dogs. But they were very, very skinny. Their coats were dulled and mangy. Their hip bones jutted out. Their ribs traced curved lines in their panting sides.

Jack looked to Moxie. "What has happened?"

We are hungry, she told him.

"You are starving! Where are all the other dogs?"

Moxie looked away.

"They died?" Jack shouted. "They *died*?"

27

Jack's reaction to seeing the sheep dogs made Moxie feel horrible. Jack's mouth had fallen open. He stood, shaking his head.

And the sheep dogs did not celebrate Jack's homecoming. They stood there, unable to do anything but stare.

Where was Blur? Moxie wondered. He could make Jack feel happy. But Blur was somewhere, away.

So Moxie barked, to get Jack's attention.

Puppies, Jack! she said. *You need to see the puppies.*

Moxie led Jack to Mother Molly and her pups.

But when Molly first saw Jack, she curled her upper lip and growled.

Jack looked to Moxie. "What is this?" he asked.

It's Molly, Moxie told him.

To Molly, she said, "This is Jack. He's the boy. Remember him? He's back. We are saved!"

"I'm sorry, Moxie," Molly said. "But I'm too weak, I'm afraid."

"Jack will save us," Moxie told Molly.

Then Moxie told Jack, *We are hungry. So hungry. We don't know what we're doing much of the time.*

Jack put his eyebrows together. His eyes showed kindness. "It's OK," he told her. "We'll get through this, together."

Jack got down onto his knees. He slowly reached the back of his hand out to Molly. Molly sniffed it, and recoiled. She sniffed it, again.

"What's that other odor?" she asked Moxie. "That's not a boy scent."

Moxie knew what she was talking about. "He must have rolled in something," she said. "Don't mind it. It will fade."

Molly let Jack pick up the puppies. Jack held each puppy to his cheek, and set it back down with its mother.

Then he petted Mollie.

"We have work to do," he told Moxie.

28

Jack knew that good sheep dogs could not make themselves kill sheep. But he also knew that he had to to get food for the sheep dogs.

Moxie had showed him her pile of the old human things. In the pile, Jack found the rusted tobacco tin where he had kept the knife. It was still there, but its blade had dulled, so he took it to the spring.

There, he dipped the blade into the water. Then he whetted the blade on a flat piece of rock. He kept dipping and whetting so that the cutting edge grew smoother and finer. When he was finished, he tested it against his thumb. *Sharp.* He and Moxie walked back to the sheep.

Jack stood and watched the sheep for a long while.

They looked pitiful. For some reason, the dogs had kept the sheep in this one place, too long. The sheep had grazed the grass down to the bare dirt, and now they stood in a dusty, hungry bunch. Luckily for the sheep, a small rivulet ran through the patch. The sheep had some muddy water, but almost no grass.

"We'll have to move them to better pasture," Jack said Moxie. "But first things first."

Moxie cocked her head. *What things?*

"You dogs need food," Jack told her. "You need it now."

I can do it, Jack thought. He had helped Cookie butcher a cow, several pigs, and even a sheep on board the *Pym*. It was hard and unpleasant, but Cookie and Jack had worked fast. They did not enjoy the killing.

Now Jack studied the flock. None of these sheep seemed an obvious sacrifice. Jack wondered, should he pick the healthiest one, for the most and best meat? Or should he choose the weakest one so that the healthier sheep survived?

"Which one?" he asked Moxie.

She didn't understand.

"I don't know, either," Jack told her. He walked around the sheep flock again. They milled as he passed them. He smelled their dirty wool and oily lanolin. Some of the sheep looked better than others. None of them looked good.

"Which one?" he asked Moxie, again.

She didn't understand. But she stood ready to help.

"OK. Be that way," Jack said. "Then it'll have to be— *uh—hmm.* This one."

Jack gripped his knife, and grabbed the biggest sheep in the flock.

But it *maaaed.* It jerked back and tore itself free. Jack was left with a handful of dirty wool.

Jack let that sheep go. Next to him stood the weakest sheep in the flock. She was an older, small ewe. She would be easy to handle, and quick to dispatch.

Jack grabbed her wool and started to pull her, but he couldn't go through with it. He could not make himself kill the weakest sheep.

"So then—what will it be?" Jack said. "Will it be the luck o' the draw? Then, at least, it won't be me who decides who lives and who dies."

Jack closed his eyes, and began roaming among the sheep. He put his hand on their backs, and moved from one to the other. Finally, he found one that didn't flinch when he grabbed it. He shook its fleece. This sheep did not move.

Jack opened his eyes. It was an old ram with a single horn.

"Sir," Jack said to the ram, "it looks like it's you."

Jack turned to Moxie, "You, stay," he commanded.

Jack grabbed the ram's horn. He pulled him away from the flock. The ram followed Jack readily. When Jack let go of the ram's horn, the ram continued to follow him.

"You're making this worse, sir," Jack said, to the ram.

The old ram followed Jack across the meadow. They walked around and behind one of the big outcrops of rock. They went out of sight of the flock and the dogs. The old ram began to eat the good grass.

"Well, sir," Jack said to the ram.

He thought, *What else can I say?*

Jack told himself that this was going to be done, and done quickly. It would be over soon, and he could feed the starving dogs. Everything would be better soon.

He just wished that he could skip to *soon* right now.

But he knew he couldn't.

"I'm sorry," he said to the old ram.

29

Moxie smelled blood.

Then Jack came back around from behind the big rocks. Jack's forelegs and front paws were bloody. He held them out, away from himself. He moved stiffly down to his place at the spring. There he scrubbed his forelegs with sand and water.

Then Jack sat back on his heels. He looked up at the sky. He looked around at the meadow. He looked thoughtful. He looked sad.

Then Jack got busy. He took off his clothes and sat down in the water. He began vigorously scrubbing himself and his clothes with the dark wet sand.

Moxie watched him, then looked back to the big rock. She left the other dogs, to go see what had happened behind it, and why the smell of blood.

30

Jack scrubbed himself at the spring.

That had been hard to do. Not so hard, physically. But mentally, it was terrible.

Still, Jack knew he could do it again.

He knew he could do a lot of things, this time on the island. He felt that he was better prepared for the island, now. He was older, for sure. He had learned a lot from Cookie. Also, having to survive that first time on the island had taught him one really good lesson—everything that you learn, anytime, will become useful, one day.

For example, he knew how to slaughter and butcher sheep. He had helped Cookie do that on board the *Pym*. And after Jack had told Cookie his stories of survival on the island, Cookie had taught him a lot of things, about all kinds of survival. The old man had lived through hotel fires, robberies, ship sinkings, and other disasters. Cookie had friends who had survived many more. Cookie was a survivor, a teacher, and a friend.

Now Jack needed to roast some of the sheep meat. But first, he relaxed and let his clothes dry some in the sun. He checked his tobacco tin, and found that there were only ten matches remaining. He would have to build one main fire, and never let it die. Cookie had taught him to burn the hardest wood, whose hot coals he could bury, and revive into fire, later on.

Jack had learned many things from Cookie about living and staying alive. He smiled now, thinking about this and thinking about his chances. This time, he and Moxie would have themselves a bully good survival.

After a while, Jack got up. He put on his clothes, and went to gather firewood, to make himself a proper home fire. He walked back past the big rocks, where he had taken the old ram. There, he got a surprise.

Moxie and other sheep dogs were behind the rocks, lying all about. Their bellies were full. They were licking their muzzles. Jack had not given them the meat yet, but they had already eaten their fills.

Only one dog was still eating. He was a young shepherd mix. Although he was still standing, his belly
looked the fullest. He glanced up from his meal. When
he saw Jack, he got all excited. He kept wagging his
tail—to say hello—but he didn't stop eating.

31

Jack and the sheep dogs moved the sheep to better pasture. All he had to do was to whistle and point, and the dogs understood what he meant.

All the dogs, that is, except the young shepherd mix, whom Jack started calling Blur. Blur was a flash and a marvel. Whenever Jack whistled to Blur and pointed—in any direction—Blur got all excited and ran straight to the cliff top. There, Blur stood shivering, waiting for a seagull to swoop past, over his head. Then he dashed after the bird's shadow, to hilarious results.

Watching Blur, Jack got an idea, which he thought would be a funny trick on a dog like Blur.

"You're going to love this," he said to Moxie.

Jack and Moxie went down to the edge of the forest,

where Jack found a tree branch with just the right bend to it. They took the branch to the top of the meadow, where he carved it into a big Australian boomerang. Jack made it three feet long and as flat as he could get it. It would need a lot of wind to fly. But if it worked, it might really soar, lazily and far.

For more fun, Jack painted his boomerang white, using white bird guano from the rocks at the cliff top. Then with charcoal from his fire, he drew on it a design of feathers, like feathers on a wing.

It still didn't look all that much like a bird. So Jack wrote a label on it.

BIRD.

Jack laughed at himself for that, because Blur couldn't read. Then for no real reason, he changed the boomerang's name to BLUR BIRD.

That made Jack roar with laughter. The words *blur bird* sounded something like the sound that Blur's ears made whenever he shook his head. His ears went *"Bllllrrr-brrrd."*

Jack showed it to Moxie. He whistled for Blur. Blur bounded down to them. Jack pointed down to the sheep, and of course Blur ran up to the cliff top. Jack and Moxie followed him. Jack waved the boomerang under Blur's nose, to get his attention. Jack thought that maybe the guano made it smell like a seagull's tail end.

After one sniff, Blur's attention returned to the ground. Blur stood, all excited and shivering, waiting for bird shadows.

"What do you think?" Jack asked Moxie.

Moxie was watching Blur. She knew what to expect.

Jack had wanted to throw the boomerang out over the meadow. That way, he could trick Blur into running a big circle around the meadow and back to Jack. But the wind was wrong for that. As usual, it was blowing in, off the ocean. Jack realized there was a chance that Blur might chase the boomerang off the cliff.

That wouldn't be good. So Jack faced out to the ocean. He remembered what the *Pym*'s crewmen Pete and Jon had taught him about throwing boomerangs. Pete and Jon sometimes held competitions, into the wind off the bow of the *Pym*.

Jack remembered his boomerang lesson. The sailors had taught him to remember the letters: *W-E-L-S-H*.

"*W* is for *wind*," Jon had told him. "To throw your boomerang, you face the wind. But you will aim a little to the right of straight into it."

"That is a fact," said Pete. "And *E* is for *elevation*.

Aim for just a few degrees above the horizon. Don't aim too high."

"*L* is for *lean*," Jon said. "You'll need to *lean* the boomerang over, like this, very slightly, to the right."

"Yes. And *S* is for *spin*," said Pete. "Cock the boomerang back in your hand, so you can make it *spin*. Otherwise, it's not a boomerang. It's just a bent stick."

"And *H* is for *hardness*," Jon said. "That's the last letter to remember. Throwing a boomerang hard is not as important as its spin."

Then Pete and Jon had argued about why you should remember *hardness*, when hardness was something you didn't want to have.

But Jack had learned his lesson. And now he rehearsed the instructions in his mind.

Then he cocked the boomerang back in his hand, to make sure it got good spin. He looked back at Blur, who was oblivious. He looked to Moxie, who was all attention. Jack then faced the cliff. He put his left foot forward, and he let the boomerang fly.

Fw-fw-fw-fw! it went.

"Beautiful!" Jack shouted.

Moxie barked.

The boomerang sailed, rolling through the air like a

wheel. It sailed out over the blue and whitecapped ocean. Then it lay over onto its side as it started its turn. And it curved, beautifully, gracefully, spinning back toward the cliff. Jack watched it, laughing and shouting. Moxie kept barking. This was working, just fine.

Then Jack realized he'd better duck, because it was coming back in, low.

Oh, no! Jack dropped to the ground and lay flat on the cliff top.

"Down, Moxie! Down!" he shouted. He pressed his cheek hard against the rocky ground.

Fw-fw-fw-fw! came the boomerang.

Fw-fw-fw-fw! It missed Moxie and sailed right above Jack, barely two feet off the ground. It clipped the hair on the top of Blur's head, and Blur was off and after it, springing like a deer.

Jack jumped up. Moxie ran after Blur.

"Ha-*hah*!" Jack laughed.

Blur chased the swooping boomerang as it spun down across the meadow. Lower, the boomerang caught an upslope wind. It climbed, made another turn, and started coming back toward Jack. Blur and Moxie altered their direction, and ran to the left, to intercept it. When the boomerang passed over a mound, Blur leaped off the mound, and caught the boomerang in his teeth.

"Ha-*hah*!" Jack exulted.

It looked more like the boomerang had caught Blur. It carried him a short distance, hanging by his teeth, spinning through the air. Then Blur crashed, right on top of Moxie.

"Ha!" Jack ran, bounding down through the meadow. He found Blur lying on his back, nearly unconscious, but with the boomerang still in his mouth. Moxie was already up. She was shaking off the effects.

"Good boy! Good boy, Blur!" Jack clapped his hands.

Blur got up, staggering happily. He dropped the boomerang, and sniffed at it, curiously.

Jack hugged Moxie. Everything was so perfect on the island that he had to think, *What could go wrong?*

The he remembered Blackburn Jukes. He remembered the fangos.

32

Moxie loved her life again. Everything was better. The sheep were getting fat. Moxie amazed herself with what she could do. And everything she did, she did for Jack.

She loved working. She loved working for Jack. She loved it so much that she woke him at dawn to get him to work her. She hurried him through his drowsy breakfasts, and harried him until he would head up toward the sheep. When they got to the sheep, she sped around the flock, to tighten it up. She wound it so tight that the sheep were bumping into one another and bleating to the skies.

This was just as she wanted them to be. She then jumped onto the back of the nearest sheep. She jumped and jumped, from sheep to sheep, clear to the other side of the flock, where Jack stood waiting.

And Moxie reported for more duty.

Where do we move them today? she asked him. *Where? Where?*

Jack laughed and said, "OK, Moxie! You can move them back to where they were—oh, I don't care. The day before yesterday."

Terrific! With the help of Boffo, Cam, and the other dogs except Blur, Moxie moved the sheep across the meadow.

Blur still hadn't figured out the whole sheep thing. But he was a great help to Moxie when it came to Jack. Jack wasn't that interested in herding sheep himself, and Blur kept him busy with his bird chases and the boomerang.

And so life was perfect for Moxie, the sheep dog. She felt she would do anything to keep it that way.

33

Life stayed good for Jack, too. The sheep dogs continued to gain back their strength. Jack and Moxie and Blur became best buddies.

Jack was better prepared this time than he had been for his first stay on the island. He was older now, and that felt good to him. He was sure he would make better decisions, and do everything better.

He knew how to get food. He would plant potatoes, radishes, carrots, and other crops. He would fish and trap. He knew there were shellfish at the beach. And he would manage the sheep. There were too few of them, now. But he and Moxie would care for them well. They would thrive and multiply. With Moxie's help, he would raise them and then harvest them, at the right times. Jack would be a proper sheep farmer.

He told himself that he was not afraid of the fangos. He felt braver, and he could see that the fangos were no longer the danger that they had once been.

So, one day, Jack went to look for them.

He made Moxie stay back in the meadow, with the mother dog and her puppies.

Moxie didn't want to stay, but he commanded her to do it.

"Guard them," he told her. "Protect them."

Jack was worried about Moxie getting near the fangos. During his first stay on the island, he and Moxie had once been surprised by fearsome fangos. Even though it was Jack, actually, who panicked and ran, Moxie felt that she had abandoned Jack. It had taken her a long time to get over her shame.

This time, Jack went alone. Once inside the forest, he headed toward its darkest region, thinking that was where he would find the fangos.

But in a long day's walk, he saw nothing—no fangos and no sign of them. He even cried out, pretending he was hurt and weak. But no fangos appeared to stalk him.

Finally, Jack turned back. He took a different way toward the meadow. This way was thicker and darker than the way he had come. When he felt he was almost back, he came upon a clearing, which felt strange the moment he entered it.

Jack could not know it, but this was the clearing where Moxie had been alone, surrounded by fangos, the year before. The clearing formed a rough circle, surrounded by thick trees, but the clearing itself was empty of any life. No brush. No grass. The air itself felt dead. The ground was covered by brown piles of dry, dead leaves. More disturbing, the place was littered all about with cracked yellow bones.

Jack picked one up. "Sheep bone," Jack whispered, when he realized what it was.

Jack stopped in the middle of the clearing. There was something *bad* about this place. It felt spooky. It smelled terrible. Jack stood still for some moments. He waited and listened. He felt as if something bad had happened here.

Or instead—a chill ran down his neck—was something bad going to happen here?

"Here?" he whispered. "Something?"

Jack slowly turned around in place. He watched the woods, but nothing was there.

Then, as he was about to resume his hike, the dead leaves on the ground around him began to move. At first, the leaves trembled, as if a breeze had disturbed them. Then Jack saw that the leaves were only rustling in certain spots, here and there, in the bigger piles of leaves. These bigger piles formed a rough circle around him.

As Jack watched, these piles began to quake. Then the piles lifted up, with the leaves spilling off on all sides.

And suddenly, where the piles had once been, there stood seven frightful fangos.

They had been lying beneath the leaves, asleep or in wait.

Jack swallowed. Slowly, he turned. The seven fangos were each about ten yards away from him. Each fango looked different from the others, yet they all looked the same. One was black. One was yellow. Another had spots. They all looked like death on four legs.

They appeared disappointed to see him. They seemed to be bored. Or perhaps they were so hungry that they couldn't show any interest. Their heads hung low. Their eyes half shut. None was facing Jack directly, at first. But now all turned toward him. They opened their mouths and began to pant. Their tongues hung out. They began to drool. Their saliva dripped, thick and ropy.

Jack felt sick to his stomach. He realized he was scared.

"You. No. No—" he said to them, with his voice low. He remembered he didn't have a weapon. He had thought he could grab a quick stick anywhere, but there was nothing, in this clearing, to fight with.

So Jack waved his arms. "Go!" he said, to the fangos. "Go! Now! *H'yah!*" He yelled at them as though they were horses.

But the fangos did not go. They did not blink.

Jack thought he should face the fangos' leader. But which one was the leader? He turned and looked at each of them, trying to decide who was the boss. During Jack's first time on the island, the fango leader had been obvious. He was the biggest, the strongest, and the most frightening fango.

But these fangos here were all starved and thin. They looked like skeletons, wearing ragged fur rugs.

As Jack slowly turned to face them all, the fangos began to act together. Whenever Jack turned, the fango right behind him took one step forward. With every complete turn, the circle of fangos grew tighter.

So Jack stopped. He turned in the opposite direction,

but the same thing happened. The circle of fangos tightened closer, although Jack never saw a fango move.

Jack stopped again, and stood still. His skin crawled, because he knew that the fango behind him was stepping closer.

Jack jumped suddenly around. He caught a fango in the act of moving.

"Hah!" Jack shouted, and pointed.

But the fango yawned, and licked its lips.

Jack's skin crawled. Again, he jumped around.

Sure enough, a fango was nearer.

What to do? What to do? Jack felt his knees weaken. His legs begin to shake.

He wondered if he would make it, if he tried to dash through the line of fangos. The weakness in his knees told him that he wouldn't.

Oh, no, he thought. *Oh, no, no, no.* Where was Moxie? He needed her. He opened his mouth to call out. But he was too scared and weak to shout.

Then, sensing his fear, all the fangos took a step toward him.

"*Oh—*" Jack uttered. Was it all over, now?

The fangos stepped closer.

Closer.

Closer still.

But it was then, and so strangely, that one of the fangos—the fango with the spots—lifted his head and looked Jack in the eyes.

It was the saddest expression Jack had ever seen, from any dog or any human, anywhere. It was full of pain, and despair, and hunger. It made Jack want to help them.

But it also unnerved and confused him all the more, to have fear and sympathy mixing inside him.

Jack asked himself, *Oh, where is Moxie?*

34

Moxie was nearer than Jack could imagine. She was racing with Blur through the brush and the trees. Jack had commanded her to stay, and she had stayed. But as she stayed, a feeling of dread grew inside her.

Jack is in danger!

She knew it. She felt it in her bones and her soul. Her desire to obey Jack had kept her in the meadow until her need to protect him had overpowered it.

Blur joined her as she dashed down through the meadow. Moxie stayed low, running intently and efficiently. Blur bounded from side to side, but he kept up with Moxie easily.

They raced through the apple orchard, into the

woodland. As they entered the darker forest, Moxie recognized where they were going. It was toward the clearing where the fangos had once surrounded her.

It was the way toward danger, so Jack was in danger!
Moxie ran faster. The brush whipped past her.

35

*W*here is Moxie? Jack wondered.

Then—*wham!*

Something slammed into one fango, and the fango went tumbling.

Wham! Something hit another fango, hard. It also went down.

Wham!

Wham!

Wham!

What was it? Jack couldn't focus on it. It was a blur.

No. It was Blur! It was the young shepherd. He didn't bite. He didn't snarl. He didn't fight. He simply slammed into the fangos at high speed, one after another.

Wham! Blur slammed the sixth fango.

And *wham!* He slammed the seventh. This one went rolling all the way out of the clearing.

Jack was astonished. He felt something leaning against his leg. It was Moxie, gazing up at him, wagging her tail.

The fangos were gone. Blur appeared again, panting. He was happy. He was shaking his head, as if trying to shake the stars out of it.

"You saved me!" Jack shouted, to Moxie and Blur.

Blur panted. Moxie wagged her tail.

Blur shook his head. *Bllllrrrbrrrds!* went the sound of his ears.

36

Moxie stayed so close to Jack that he tripped over her twice on their way back to the meadow.

When they reached home, Jack got down on the ground and rolled around with the puppies. He carried sticks in his mouth. He frolicked along on his forelegs and knees as the puppies gamboled about him. Jack even picked up the pups in his mouth, holding them by the scruffs of their necks. What a clown Jack was! Not even Blur could be as funny.

Jack made his happy boy-barking sounds. He barked around the puppies. He barked at Blur. He barked at Blur until he fell down, barking. Then Jack rolled onto his back and barked and barked.

Moxie felt nothing but happiness.

37

Time passed. But for Jack, it seemed as if time had stopped.

Or it seemed as if time had gone far away.

This might be because time is change. Or because time is a way that people sense change. And nothing could change anything between Jack and Moxie.

So, for Jack, it was almost as if there was no time. Or, as Jack put it, there was tons of time.

But wait a minute, Jack said to himself. *Tons of time?*

That made Jack wonder. *Or is time weightless?*

But time had once seemed a heavy load, in that year that Jack had spent without Moxie.

This weight of his thinking now made Jack shake his head.

"No," he said, aloud. "Time is like the air."

Time must be like the breeze. It blew back and forth. Fast or slow, time was always moving. Time was free and priceless. Jack breathed and enjoyed it.

But one dewy morning, as they watched the sun rise, Jack idly asked Moxie, "What is time, really?"

Jack didn't expect an answer. But Moxie turned and looked at him, with her intense collie eyes, one blue and one brown.

Her blue eye told him, *Time is worry.*

Her brown eye said, *We have no worries.*

"I see," Jack said, and he tried to understand.

So then, he thought, *if worry is gone, then time is gone, too?*

Jack shook his head again, and he let all his thought go. He laughed, empty-minded and worry-free.

But time returned, on a still afternoon. It happened when Jack suddenly wondered: *What of Blackburn Jukes?*

That made him wonder: How long had it been?

Blackburn Jukes, Jack thought. *Blackburn Jukes.*

Time started ticking for Jack, again.

The very next day, Jack stood in the meadow and watched Moxie and the other dogs moving the sheep. He noticed several of the dogs stop and raise their noses to sniff at the air.

Something is different, they signaled. *Something in the air.*

Jack tried to smell it, too. He couldn't. He looked around. There was nothing to see. But half an hour later, he saw something. It was smoke, rising above the thick woods, in the direction of Dutchman's Cove. It was a leaning, white column of smoke, like smoke puffing up from someone's chimney.

Something has changed, the dogs kept signaling. They grouped the sheep more closely, in case this something that was different was something bad.

"What is it, Moxie?" Jack called down to his dog.

It's smoke. Moxie was watching it. *But it's not your smoke.*

Jack knew if the smoke was from Dutchman's Cove, it had to be due to Blackburn Jukes.

Moxie looked at him with her bright, wise eyes of two separate colors. Each eye held a question.

Is it good? the brown eye asked him.

Is it bad? the blue eye wondered.

Jack realized that he didn't know any better than Moxie did.

Then he had the sudden feeling that whenever he was talking with Moxie, he was really talking to himself.

And so what, if that's what was happening? Maybe, when you have a really good friend, both of you can think the same thoughts at the same time. You don't have to think different thoughts. And maybe—

And maybe—

Jack held his next thought.

Tick, tick, tick. Jack could almost hear time.

He shook his head, to dislodge the feeling. Here he was again, *thinking* too much. It was better to be like a dog. A dog could smell old things, and sense new things. That's how Moxie did her thinking. Jack should sense the whole world and take it in, as a whole, rather than think it apart, into little bits.

"I ought to be more like you," he said to Moxie.

Moxie looked at him directly. *Maybe you already are.*

Jack laughed at that thought. But the smoke kept puffing into the sky, above Dutchman's Cove. What did it mean?

Maybe it meant merely that Jukes was down there, living.

Or maybe it meant that Jukes was up to something, that Jukes was into something that wasn't good for Jack and the sheep dogs.

Jack watched the smoke for the rest of the day.

For the rest of that day, time flew past. Clouds flew fast. Birds flew faster.

Jack took some distraction in watching Blur trying to catch seagulls. But he kept thinking about the morning's smoke rising out of Dutchman's Cove.

A thought popped into his mind.

Maybe it's a harbinger, he thought.

Then Jack realized that he didn't know what the word *harbinger* meant. He wondered if—without people around him to talk with—his supply of words might one day dry up.

Big deal, he thought. *Who needs time? Who needs people? And without people, who needs words?*

Jack had been using words less and less. When he talked to himself aloud, the sound of his voice sometimes irritated him now. He didn't talk much to Moxie, not in words, anyway. He just thought what he thought, and his dog understood. It was a good way for them to be—almost as if they were two dogs.

But he kept remembering the smoke. A harbinger?

Jack put his hands over his ears. He watched Blur in action as the dog surprised himself again. The dog was a comic, always surprised, and always delighted. With his hands over his ears, Jack tried to laugh. But his laughter sounded odd, like somebody else's.

That night, very late, another storm blew in. Thunder rumbled across the meadows. The dogs worked hard to calm the sheep. The lightning began as flashing sheets of light, spreading from one side to the other of the sky. But soon, the lightning focused into one area, over Dutchman's Cove.

Jack sat and watched the storm with growing awe. Storms had never acted quite this way before. This one seemed to be attracted—pulled in, almost—to Dutchman's Cove. There, the lightning blinked. It shuddered. It flashed. Then all its energy seemed to contract to one spot.

It became a lasting point of light, glowing in the clouds.

Jack looked over at Moxie. Was she seeing this, too?

She was fascinated by it. Her head was tipped to one side.

"How about that?" Jack asked her. He looked back at the storm.

And just in time. A great bolt of sky fire shot down to the earth.

It happened in silence. All became dark. And then—

BARRRRROOOOOOOOOM!!!

Thunder knocked Jack onto his back.

Moxie *yiked*. She spun around. She sped off, up the meadow, to help the other dogs with the sheep.

The thunder echoed and reechoed for more than a minute. Jack sat up. He rubbed his shoulders and shivered.

Jack watched the air above the cove. There was something different in the air. Above Dutchman's Cove, there was a different kind of glow. There was no wind. A *ruru* owl began to hoot. The owl sounded like it was saying, *"Mo' poor. Mo' poor."* Jack felt drawn toward the cove. He knew he had to go down to see about Jukes.

39

The rest of that night, Moxie kept guard.

But as soon as the storm was over, the sheep forgot all about it. They were sheep, after all. They settled and forgot that there had even been a storm. Then they slept, as sheep sleep. They looked like dim dream scraps of wool, like night lint, caught in the meadow.

All night, Moxie stood guard. At dawn, she heard Jack's whistle. Her ears turned toward it. But it wasn't his best whistle. It wasn't Jack's sure, sharp, two-note whistle that usually said to her, "I'm happy to be alive!"

This whistle was hedged. It was a short string of slightly sour notes. It said, "Well—? Well—?"

Moxie ran to where Jack stood, lower in the meadow.

He was looking over the old apple orchard, toward the forest below it.

Uh-oh, Moxie thought. Jack was looking toward the place where the big lightning had happened the night before.

"Well—?" Jack was saying. "Well—?"

Then he shrugged and he said, "Well, Moxie? Come on."

Jack took a step, but then stopped. He turned, and looked all around, at the meadow and the sheep, and then back down at Moxie. He looked again toward the woods, and then up at the sky above them. Moxie saw there were puffs of smoke above the horizon again.

Is that it, Jack? she wondered. *The smoke?*

Jack nodded.

"What do you think?" Jack said to her. He had a worried look.

I don't think we should, Moxie thought, but Jack didn't sense it.

The boy and dog slowly walked through the orchard and into the lower woods. Jack took the lead and Moxie followed, watchfully. She sniffed the air for fangos. She caught their odor, here and there, but the scents were so weak and so pitifully rank that she felt sorry for the fangos, just a little.

She wondered. What would the world be like without any fangos at all? Would the dogs' world be better? Or do dogs need there to be some danger, in order to keep them on the alert?

Moxie wanted to ask Jack, but she didn't know how to ask the question. Maybe she should take Jack and go show him some weakened fangos. He might know what to do about them.

Jack was walking through the woods carefully. He was trying to be quiet. Of course, he was a human, and he was clumsy. Twigs snapped as he stepped on them. Bushes rattled as he pushed through them. Jack was a noisemaker, for sure.

Also, Jack had begun to smell anxious. Moxie didn't like the worried odor. On Jack, it stank. Worse, it made her worry, too.

They walked a long time. Finally they came to a grassy opening in the trees. Jack stopped and watched it. There was an obvious path across it. The path would be a quieter way for Jack to walk. But Jack stood thinking, as though he was not sure they should cross.

Then he shrugged his shoulders and walked into the clearing.

But something wasn't right. Moxie stayed back, watching.

Then all of a sudden, a tall, two-legged creature stepped right in front her.

Moxie startled. She slunk low. She put her chin on the ground. She rolled her eyes up at the creature. What was it? It was big. Moxie sniffed. It was male. Was he human? Moxie watched him, wanting no confrontation.

The creature wore clothing. That certainly seemed human. He put his forepaw to his face and stroked some hair that grew below his nose. He was much taller than Jack. He looked more powerful. He seemed to wear a collar made of fur. Moxie smelled the maleness and an odd smoke smell, and another alien, bitter scent.

This odor was remarkable. It was like old urine. Ammonia. It bit her in her nose. It was the same bothersome stink that Jack had had stuck in his hair that day he had come back to the sheep dogs. It wasn't a human scent. It was animal, but alien.

The tall creature stared down at Moxie with two frightful eyes. The eyes were not identical, but not in the way sheep dogs' eyes are sometimes different. One eye showed cunning. The other seemed dead. But, somehow, it glowed.

Moxie looked through the creature's legs, out into the clearing. Jack had kept walking, unaware. He was now on the other side of the clearing, disappearing into the woods.

Should Moxie bark? She wanted to, but she couldn't. Her throat had gone tight.

Should she run to Jack? Yes! That was it. She tensed and got ready.

But then, the creature spoke.

He said, "Dog."

He spoke! The thing spoke, like Jack did! He must be a human! He was a human, like Jack was! Oh, good! Then he must be wonderful.

And since he was bigger than Jack was, then he must be a man. What a relief! Moxie rose from the ground. This man had to be good, because Jack was so good. This very big man had to be very good.

But Moxie suddenly had a sharp memory of the men who had come and kidnapped Jack off the island the first time, after the big war with the fangos. One of them had left a scent of sweet smoke.

Was this one of those men?

So what to do? What should she do? Moxie prepared to chase after Jack.

But the man spoke again. "Hello, dog."

Then strangely, he started barking softly, in a low throaty voice. "Ha-hah. Ha-HAH. Ha-hah-hah-HAH!"

It wasn't a happy bark, but it seemed amused, so this man was probably happy.

That was good, Moxie thought. At least, she hoped it was good.

"Ha-hah. Ha-HAH. Ha-hah-hah-HAH!"

Moxie watched as the man barked. Then an absolutely unbelievable thing happened.

The man grew a second head.

Moxie quailed. She shrank in horror, as a new, smaller head poked itself around the man's first head, and it looked straight down at Moxie.

What was it? This second head was black, with white and gray specks. Its fur looked like it had been partly burned. It had pointed ears. Its small round eyes had thin black pupils. They were more like sheep's eyes than they were like dogs'.

The second head opened its mouth. Its teeth had the sharpest points that Moxie had ever seen. Then it hissed! It hissed. Like nothing Moxie had ever heard.

"Hssssssssst!"

Then the head disappeared behind the first head.

But it reappeared on the other side.

What? This head wasn't connected to the man. It was separate. It was part of a smaller creature, which had been lying on the back of the man's neck. The creature now stepped out onto the man's shoulder. It waved its tail like a snake waves its tail as it slithers. It looked to be the size of a newborn lamb.

It didn't act like a lamb. It hissed at Moxie.

"Hssssssssst!"

Moxie growled back at it.

The small creature arched its back and hissed again.

Suddenly, Moxie caught its full scent. It was the odor that had been in Jack's hair, sharp and ammonia-like. It was totally and absolutely *other*. Moxie's hair stood up on her neck. She did not like this creature. She wanted to chase it.

But the man barked. "Ha-hah!"

"Dog," he said. He fixed Moxie to the ground with his scary eyes.

Under their power, Moxie grew confused. So like the good dog she was, Moxie did what a good dog often does when it is confused and intimidated. Moxie rolled onto her back. She bared her belly to him, to show the man that she meant him no harm.

"That's a good doggie," the man said.

And he put his foot down onto her throat.

Gulp! What? Moxie thought. *What?*

Panic began. Moxie went as limp as she could, to prove to the man that she was no threat.

But the man pressed his foot down a little more.

Then he pressed a lot more. Moxie could not breathe. She tried to pull out, but the man had her pinned. She struggled. She was unable to move. So she lay there, as still as she could.

She rolled her eyes, to look up at the man. He was baring his teeth and shaking his head. He pressed his foot onto her throat harder. Moxie's heart hammered and her lungs worked hard, but no air would come into them.

"Ha-hah! Ha-hah-hah!" the man barked evilly.

Moxie's heart began to flutter, and her lungs trembled. She weakened. She trembled. Black spots popped into her vision. The spots began to spin around the man's head. They swirled into one big, vanishing pool.

Then the man took his foot off her throat.

Moxie sucked in a lungful of air, but she didn't move. She lay as still and limp and submissive as she could.

Why had the man done that? Had he wanted to show her that he had the power?

Moxie knew that. She feared him. He could be the leader, for now. When Jack came back, they would see.

But then the tall man barked again his strange bark. "Ha-hah! Ha-ha-*hah!*" He bent back one of his long legs.

And he kicked Moxie.

Thwump!

He kicked her. He kicked her. He kicked her again. When Moxie looked up, the strange creature was barely hanging on to the man's back.

Then the man kicked Moxie so hard that she flew high into the air. She twisted over once, bounced off a tree, and landed, crumpled, on her side.

"Ha-*HAH!*" the man barked evilly.

"Hssssssssst!" the creature hissed.

Then the man barked again, in a cruel and callous tone. He was growling at her, cursing her, pointing and ordering Moxie to leave.

Slowly, in pain, Moxie rose to her feet. Her gut ached. Her ribs stung. She could only breathe half breaths. This man was bad, an evil human being.

And where was Jack? Where had he gone?

The bad man took a step toward Moxie, to threaten

another kick. Then he turned and walked away, in the direction Jack had gone. The creature on his shoulder hissed back at Moxie.

Moxie limped back through the woods, toward the high meadow. As she went, she wondered, what did this mean? She was a dog. She was hurt and bewildered. What does a real dog do when it has been hurt and abused?

Jack followed the trail through the woods, down toward the cove. When the trail entered the defile, he remembered the old snare that had snaked around his ankle and hung him, dangling upside down. Jack walked more cautiously. He wasn't going to let himself get trapped again.

The snare had been right about here. Jack slowed even more. Where exactly had it been? The trail was covered with leaves. Jack stopped and looked up. He saw bent-over treetops.

Carefully, Jack took two more light steps. He was about to take another, but something made him stop again. It was a danger sense. He felt it, right here. Jack held his breath. He did not move.

This was where the snare had been set, Jack felt sure. He looked all around without moving his feet. He saw leaves, trees, rocks, brush. He looked up the steep slope beside him, and he saw the large boulders poised precariously above the trail.

He looked at the trees again. He saw nothing that—

But wait.

There! Jack now saw that one bowed young tree had a thin line tied to its top. It looked almost like spider's silk. He could see it only when the sunlight caught it, just so. The line ran, taut and quivering, from the treetop down through branches to the ground. There, it disappeared beneath leaves at the side of the trail, barely one yard away from where Jack now stood.

Jack swallowed, hard. He looked at his feet. He was standing on leaves. They hid whatever might be in the trail with him. Jack took a deep breath. He took one big step backward. Then he knelt, and carefully, he began lifting the leaves off the trail.

One by one, he lifted off the leaves. He uncovered a noose, a simple loop of line with a slipknot. It was spread out in a circle, two feet in diameter. The line was amazingly thin and looked very strong. It must have been made from silk.

Carefully, Jack picked up the snare line between his forefinger and thumb, and he lifted it out of the leaves. He followed along it, off the trail into the brush. He found where it was tied to a trigger, which someone had fashioned from a forked stick. The trigger stick had been placed into a notch in a stake, which was stuck deep into the ground. This snare was all set and ready to trip.

"Jukes," Jack whispered. He nodded and whistled.

His whistling reminded him of Moxie. He looked back, but she wasn't there.

He called quietly, "Moxie—?"

Perhaps Moxie had sensed the danger and stayed back. Jack's senses were surely heightened. The snare had frightened him, but his finding it now encouraged him. He felt ready to go on.

But Moxie? Jack waited, but she didn't come. She had seemed reluctant to follow him earlier. Would she come along later? Jack half hoped that she would not.

Jack looked back down at the snare. It was clearly meant to trap a human. Its trigger looked too stout to be sprung by a small dog.

And springing it now might warn Jukes that Jack was nearby. So Jack decided to leave it set, and to go on.

But he looked back again for Moxie. Then he looked at the snare and its trigger stick.

If Moxie were to trip the snare, there was no telling what bad things might happen to her.

Jack looked back again. What should he do?

Well, heck. Jack shrugged, and he kicked at the trigger stick.

ZssssSCHWHOOMP! It flew up. The line yanked out of Jack's hand. The young tree straightened and shook. Its top waved back and forth through the other treetops. The snare line zipped back and forth above them, like a fisherman's line. *Sh-wish. Sh-wish. Sh-wish.*

Jack studied other treetops that seemed to be bent over, too. More snares? Likely. He thought of Moxie again.

"Jukes be damned," Jack said.

He knelt and picked up a broken tree limb. Then he set the leafy end of the limb on the ground. *This will be my vine sweeper,* he thought. And he began sweeping the limb along the ground in front of him. Jack began walking along the trail toward the cove.

Shfwoomp! The limb was snatched out of his hands and yanked up into the trees.

"Aha," Jack said. He picked up another limb and continued.

Shfwoomp!

And another.

Shfwoomp!

And another. Jack sprang five snares before he got out of the defile. There, the trail petered out again, and he continued on.

Soon, Jack was near Dutchman's Cove. He carefully picked his way around the bog. He entered the grove of giant kauri trees. Their tops waved slightly beneath a light breeze. Jack listened for sounds that might mean Jukes. He didn't hear any. He didn't know whether that should make him feel better or not.

Jack decided that it didn't make him feel better. He turned to look back for Moxie again. Where was she? Maybe he should go back?

Then Jack noticed what seemed to be a newly made path into the grove. It was about thirty yards to the side, coming from the bog. Jack walked over to it. The path looked like it had been made by dragging something heavy along the ground.

The path started somewhere deep in the bog. It led past Jack, toward the center of the grove, where the tree house and the strange cellar were.

Jack followed the path carefully. He was going that way, anyway. But the path stopped within a few yards. At its end was a big—*something*. A big ball of something. It was the size of a cantaloupe. It had the color and the glow of—

Of what? Jack asked himself.

Of maple syrup. It looked like a big ball of hardened syrup. Jack stared at it for a moment. How strange it was. Then he realized that the big ball must be a great globe of kauri amber, like the amber he had found in the cellar, his first day back on the island.

But the amber in the cellar had not been anywhere near this big.

Or this heavy. Or with this much glow. This amber was enchanted. It made Jack whistle. He stepped back, to look at it.

It did, didn't it? It seemed to glow.

"Imagine!" Jack said. He took another step back.

And—*fwoomp!*

Something had dropped down over Jack's head. Everything went dark.

"Hey!" Jack yelled. But his voice was muffled, even to himself. Jack pushed at what covered him. It was a heavy cloth. He seemed to be caught in a big, rough heavy sack.

"Hey! Hey!" he shouted, but his voice was muted.

"Hey!" he shouted. He pushed at the cloth. He tried to turn, but couldn't.

He tried to walk, but he couldn't, because his movements made the sack cinch around his ankles, as tight as a noose.

Oh, not again, Jack thought.

And then—*sschlllllip!*

Jack's feet were yanked out from under him. He fell over, wrapped inside the sack. He struggled, but he was dragged along the ground and hoisted into the air. He hung, bouncing, upside down.

"Hey!" Jack struggled. He felt like a moth in a cocoon that would not come open.

Then hands grabbed his shoulders. Then the hands sent him spinning, around and around, inside the dark sack.

Jack got dizzy. Hearty laughter circled around him as the sack spun.

"Ha-ha-hah!"

It was Jukes.

Faster and faster, Juke's laughter spun around him—
"Ha-ha-hah!

    "Ha-ha-hah!

        "Ha-ha-*HAH*!

            "Ha-ha-*HAH*!

                "Ha-ha-hah!

            "Ha-ha-hah!

        "Ha-ha-*HAH*!

    "Ha-ha-*HAH*!

"Ha-ha-HAH!"

And: "Ha-*hah*! Now you'll be my digger!"

Jack grew dizzier. "Moxie!" he shouted. "Moxie! Moxie!"

He shouted her name until he got so dizzy that he had to grit his teeth or he would throw up. Jack spun in Jukes's trap until he passed out.

42

Moxie dragged herself back through the woods, up toward the meadow and the other sheep dogs.

She felt dazed and defeated. She felt like an un-dog, a nondog, a nothing at all. She had been kicked and beaten by a creature who must have been a man. Worse, she must have been abandoned by her own boy, Jack.

She felt all the sad feelings. She felt all the low emotions, which dogs feel ten times lower than a human does.

Why hadn't Jack come back? Why wouldn't he save her?

What had she done wrong? Why had Jack gone on without her?

Was it something that dogs do not know about humans?

Jack was the only human she had ever known. And Jack was good. Wasn't he?

Yes! Moxie thought, as strongly as she could. Jack most certainly was good.

So then. This must be Moxie's own fault?

Yes. It must be.

That made Moxie feel better, that it wasn't Jack's fault. But it made Moxie feel worse at the same time. She went back into her memories, to the time of the beating. The kicking and the beating. She felt it all again. Moxie felt it in her flesh and in her bones.

She saw the image in her mind. She saw the face of that man beating her. He was evil. He was hurtful. He was horrible and mean. Moxie could not bear the ugliness of the bad man's image. But she could not get it out of her mind.

She felt guilty, sad, strange, dizzy. She felt so confused that she tried and she tried to remember Jack's loving face. But when she managed to recall Jack's face, she saw it as the face on the man who had beaten her.

For one second—in Moxie's memory—it was Jack, beating Moxie!

No! Moxie shook her head, until her ears beat her face. She rubbed her nose with both paws. She chewed dirt. She bit a rock. She made herself sneeze. She sneezed, and sneezed again. But she could not shake out this awful idea. She could not sneeze her way free from these feelings of shame.

Moxie started moving again. She padded along slowly. But she was moving only because of a dog's deep instinct. She felt she needed to go back to her own pack of dogs, up in the high meadow.

When she was nearly through the forest, Moxie entered a clearing. She stopped for a moment. This seemed a dead space, and morbid. The clearing smelled strongly of *fango*.

Then Moxie realized what this place was. It was the clearing where she had once been alone, surrounded by fangos. And it was the clearing where she and Blur had rescued Jack.

It was the fango lair, and deadly dangerous. She should go around it. But Moxie's low emotions did not let her be careful. She started to cross the clearing.

As she did, she smelled every fango, all seven of them. She smelled which one was which—black, yellow, and spotted. She smelled where each fango had stood when they had surrounded her.

When she reached the center of the clearing, she smelled something else. What was this? Moxie stopped.

It was Jack that she smelled.

Jack's scent was days old, but it was strong enough to read.

This scent did not have any of Jack's happiness. It was the scent of Jack in fear.

Moxie shivered as she examined his scent. Jack had been terrified, exactly here.

As painful as it was to do it, Moxie inhaled Jack's scent memory, and got the event into order. First she smelled Jack being startled. Then she smelled Jack surrounded. Then she smelled Jack encircled by the pack of fangos.

Jack's scent described the circle of seven fangos as they had closed in on Jack. They had drooled and panted. Moxie smelled their hunger. Had they expected to eat Jack's flesh?

Moxie sniffed at the ground for the answer. But then—

She smelled Blur! She smelled Blur, and then she smelled herself. They were coming to Jack's rescue. *Wham!* Blur slammed a fango. *Wham! Wham! Wham!* Blur slammed the others.

Jack was saved! Happiness began to seep back into Moxie's brain. She started to sniff for more good memories of Jack.

But then Moxie noticed something that snapped her mind back into the present.

What was this? She looked up.

This was bad. Moxie was again surrounded by fangos, herself.

She shook her head, bewildered. The fangos stood on all sides. They watched her. They nodded. Was that simply hunger—or was that murder in their eyes?

At first, Moxie stood still. Then she let her head drop lower. She raised the hackles on her back. She bared her teeth at the fangos.

But then she remembered Jack, who had also been surrounded by fangos. What had really happened around him then? What had happened with Jack? Moxie sniffed the ground, trying to bring back Jack's scent memory.

But his scent was now mixed with the stench of the fangos. It changed Moxie's thinking. It led Moxie to think that Jack might have made some pact with the fangos.

Had Jack somehow changed on that day?

And was that why Jack left Moxie and went off to be with the bad man?

The fangos circled Moxie, closer and closer, with lowered heads.

Moxie snarled as she watched them. But she began to feel low again. She felt worthless and empty, as though she was nothing. She began to wonder: *What is the use?* What were her reasons for living?

As the fangos circled, Moxie began to see her life as a circle. First Jack had come into her life. Then Jack had been gone. Then Jack had come back. Now Jack was gone again.

And so what was the use?

The fangos circled Moxie with their patience and long hunger. One fango drooled a yellowy rope of thickened drool. It dragged and stretched, and broke off on the ground.

Moxie raised her head, one last time, as a true sheep dog.

So this is it? she wondered. She got herself ready to fight.

"Do you want me?" she asked the fangos.

43

You'll be my digger," Jukes had told Jack on the sea, in the lifeboat.

"You'll be my digger," Jukes had told Jack while Jack was swinging in the snare.

"You'll be my digger," Jukes told Jack again now as he threw Jack down into the cellar.

Jukes was humming as he slammed shut the cellar door. Jack was left in the dank dark. He could see nothing. All was black. Jack waited for his eyes to adjust to the dark. But they could not. It was so very dark.

"Hey!" Jack shouted, out of aggravation. But this dungeon muffled his voice, except where it echoed off hard objects.

After a while, Jack began to feel his way around the

cellar. He touched treasures and trifles, trying to guess what they were. Gold coins, iron chains, the stuffed armadillo. When Jack found what felt to be a blanket, he wrapped himself up in it, and he lay down and slept.

Jack slept. He woke. He slept. He woke. But every time he woke, it was always pitch-black.

Hours later. A day later? More? Less? The cellar door was suddenly thrown open. Bright daylight burst in and battered Jack's eyes. Jack held his hands up to shield them.

A humming filled the cellar, followed by an actor's voice.

"Come out! Come out, wherever you are! Ha-ha-ha-ha!"

It was Blackburn Jukes.

Then Jukes's humming flowed again into the cellar, like water. The humming flowed in, and flooded the entire chamber. It set Jack's teeth to buzzing. It almost made him sick. Combined with the bright light, the humming overwhelmed him.

"Come out! Come out!" Jukes sang, like an opera singer.

Jack stood. Shielding his eyes, he stumbled up through the doorway and into full sunlight.

He was still wrapped in what he had thought was a blanket. But it was the bloody battle flag of the republic of Ecuador. Jack dropped it and stared at the blood in sudden disgust.

Jukes pointed at the dried blood. He laughed. "Mr. President!" he joked. "It appears you have been shot!"

Jukes laughed and bowed, as if being applauded for his act. When he straightened back up, in his hand was a pistol.

It was huge, a six-shooter Navy revolver.

"Meet my persuader," he said to Jack.

Jukes held the pistol as if it weighed nothing. But in Jack's eyes, it weighed a ton.

"Have you eaten breakfast?" Jukes asked Jack. "No? Well, tomorrow, be sure that you have. Because from now on, you dig. You dig for amber, for me."

Do you want me?" Moxie asked, ready for the end.

But the fangos did not answer her.

Moxie watched them. "Do you want me?" she asked them again.

They didn't answer. They circled Moxie. Their slack, mangy hides hung from their ribs.

Their despair washed through Moxie. For a moment, she forgot her will to fight. She even imagined lying down—letting the fangos do what they would do. She thought she was like them. She was nothingness, too. Without Jack, she could never be a true dog again. Shouldn't she just let it end now, like this, and get it over with?

At that point, the drooling fango coughed and swallowed. He licked his slavering jowls. He laughed a wheezy, hollow laugh. And in an odd way, he seemed to be trying to speak. In a choppy, stuttering way, he managed to say, *"J-j-j-juh-join uh-uh-us."*

Moxie looked away, at another fango. It looked stupid and mean. But it was nodding a slow, bobbing nod. It also was trying to say, *J-j-join us.*

Join us?

Yes. *"J-j-j-join us,"* all the fangos were now saying. *"H-h-help-uh-us. H-h-help us. HELP US!"*

How could this be happening? Moxie summoned her last strength. She curled her upper lip. She snarled at the fangos. Through her pain and shame, she bared all her teeth and let them hear her best growl.

"G-r-r-r-r-r-r-r-r—" Moxie snarled.

"H-help us," the fango tried to say again.

Moxie growled, but she listened to them. Slowly, she understood.

Blackburn Jukes meant it when he said there would be
no breakfast. He patted his jacket pocket, where the pistol made a heavy bulge.

"It's my persuader," Jukes said. "Don't make me
use it."

He handed Jack a shovel. Then he pushed Jack and
marched him through the grove and out into the
kauri bog.

Jukes had left behind all his charm on board the
Pym. He only used it now to charm himself. He sneered
at Jack. He spoke in commands.

"Go that way. Don't step there. Don't stop. Keep
walking. Not there. Go that way."

The sodden bog had puddles everywhere. The remains of kauri trunks stuck up at odd angles. Jack and Jukes stepped carefully through it, taking a winding route.

Finally, "Don't step there!" Jukes shouted. "I said, don't step—!"

But Jack had stepped into a soft patch of bog. He sank past his ankle. When he tried to pull his foot out, a strong suction held it down fast.

Jukes laughed at Jack's problem, but he wasn't amused.

"The bog has got you," he said. His voice turned weary. "Now what are you going to do?"

Jack pulled up on his foot, but the bog gave a loud *slurp*. It held his foot tight.

"What do I do?" Jack asked.

"What?" Jukes said. "You do as I say. First hand me the shovel—no, not that end. The handle end. You hold the blade. There. Now sit down, and lean toward me as I pull."

Jack pulled. Jukes pulled. The bog let go of Jack's foot.

"Now get up and go," Jukes said, "where I tell you to go."

The day was hot and quiet. Insects buzzed by.

Occasionally a frog croaked, but no birds sang and no breeze blew.

Jukes mentioned the silence. "All the better," he said, "to listen for the sound of the amber."

They stopped at a place that looked the same as all the others. Jukes picked up a straight pole that had been left there, before. The point of the pole was tipped with iron. Jukes plunged the pole into the soft bog, straight down. He seemed to listen. He shook his head. He took a step and plunged the pole into the bog again. He listened. He shook his head.

He did this four times. Then he handed the pole to Jack.

"Now, before you dig, you *plumb*," Jukes told Jack. "You plumb for the amber. For bog gum. You do it over and over, and over, again."

And so, for hours, Jack probed the bog for amber. Occasionally, he hit something. It made a soft, dull *thonk*. Jukes had him dig down to it with the shovel. It sometimes took an hour to dig to it, but it was only an old kauri root.

"That's another lesson for you," Jukes told him. "Remember what that sound was not. That wasn't am-

ber. That's not what you want. You're listening for amber. Get going." Jukes patted the pistol in his pocket.

Jack picked up the pole and plumbed for amber.

Twice, Jack struck something that sounded a little
different. Was it amber? Jukes shrugged. He made Jack
dig to find out.

Both times, it was just more kauri root wood.

"You are worse than I feared you'd be," Jukes told
Jack. "You need to learn to see—to see with your ears."

Jukes reached into a jacket pocket. He pulled out a
black scarf.

46

H-help us!" the fangos said.

But Moxie took her chance. She dashed through the line of fangos. They did not try to stop her. Moxie ran out of the clearing, through the forest, and through the orchard. She burst into the meadow and into the bright summer sunlight. She raced up to the flock of sheep, where the sheep dogs stood guard.

"Hi, Moxie!" Cam called.

"What's happening?" asked Boffo.

Moxie stopped. She stood facing them, catching her breath.

"What's up?" Cam asked.

Moxie looked at him, still panting. Cam looked healthy and whole. So did all of the sheep dogs, now that

Jack had come back to the island and provided them with food.

"Hey. Where's the boy?" Cam asked.

"Yeah! Where's the boy?" asked Boffo.

Blur came bounding up. He shook his ears. "Where's my friend Jack?" he asked.

"Yeah. We're getting hungry," the sheep dogs told her. "Where's our Jack? Where is he?"

47

Jukes was humming as he shook open the black scarf.

He said, "You'll need to see what my blind digger saw."

Jukes tied the scarf over Jack's eyes. Each time he pulled the knot tighter behind Jack's head, Blackburn Jukes hummed a little louder.

For Jack, everything became as black as in the cellar. But it was a black that was filled with Jukes's buzzing humming. The humming grew louder and louder.

Then suddenly the humming stopped. But the blackness stayed.

All was silence. At first, Jack heard nothing but himself swallowing. He listened. He heard nothing. Without sight and without sound, he began to feel dizzy. He felt like he was about to fall down.

But slowly he began to detect faint sounds around him. He heard the buzz of a fly. The breath of the breeze in his ears.

Then Jukes spoke.

"Jack."

It was as if Jukes was speaking inside Jack's head.

"All right now, Jack," Jukes said.

Jack turned his head, left and then right, to try to get a fix on Jukes's voice.

But Jukes must have been standing directly behind Jack, because Jukes's voice filled Jack's head.

Inside Jack's head, Jukes's voice said, "Now. You really start plumbing. *Move!*"

Unsteady, Jack took one step on the bog. He lost his balance. He used the pole to catch himself. He waited, half dizzy, half frightened. He took another step.

"PLUMB!" Jukes's voice swelled, full in Jack's head.

Jack spread his feet. He lifted the pole. And he plunged the pole's metal tip down into the bog.

He felt nothing at all. He heard nothing but the slide of the pole into the bog.

Jack pulled up the pole. He took one step. He plunged it down again.

Nothing.

And again. Nothing.

And nothing, again. Nothing. Nothing. Nothing.

Then suddenly: *Thonk.*

Thonk? Jack was sure that was just wood.

"It's wood," he said, not that certain of what he said.

"Well, bully!" said Jukes. "Good job. Now find me my amber."

Jack kept stepping and plunging. Nothing. Nothing. Nothing. *Thonk!* More wood. Then nothing, nothing, nothing.

Then suddenly, *Thack!*

Thack?

"That's got to be some amber," Jack said.

"Excellent, my boy," Jukes said.

Jack smiled. He reached to take off his blindfold. But he heard a dull, metal *click.*

"That's your pistol," Jack said.

"*Hmm?*" Jukes said. "Your hearing is improving."

The shovel was thrust into Jack's hands. He dug for almost an hour, down to where the globe of amber lay buried in the bog.

It took another half hour to dig the amber loose. Jack started to lift it, but Jukes grabbed him by his shoulders and dragged him from the hole.

Jack heard Jukes jump down into the hole. Then Jukes started laughing.

"Ha-ha-hah! Ha-ha-*hah*!"

Jukes sounded more than exultant. Jack took a chance. He lifted his blindfold off one eye, to snatch a peek.

Jack was surprised that it was that late in the day. The light was dim. But Jack's eyes were used to the dark. They beheld an astonishing sight.

"Ha-ha-hah!"

Blackburn Jukes was standing in the hole, waist-deep. He held a big amber globe in the crook of his left arm. He was caressing the amber with his right hand. As he did so, the globe glowed orange. Blue sparks flowed around the edges of Jukes's body, like a fluid. Jukes's hair stood out like needles. His odd right eye glowed. It looked as though it had an electric fire inside it.

"Ha-ha-hah!"

As Jukes laughed, on his shoulder stood his cat, Scorch. Scorch's back arched high. The electricity surged around the cat, too. It seemed to jump, in blue sparks, between the tips of his ears.

Then Scorch noticed Jack. He hissed. He hissed blue-fire spittle.

Then Jukes saw Jack. But the scene was so powerful that Jack could not put his blindfold back down.

Jukes glared at Jack. He reached slowly for his pistol, which was lying near the hole, on the ground.

Jukes touched the gun, and—

BLAM!

Jack put his hands over his ears. The pistol was spinning like a pinwheel on the ground. As it slowed, smoke rose from its barrel in a wavy blue spiral.

Jukes, too, was watching the pistol slowly spin to a stop. His blue sheen of sparks had disappeared. He set the amber down and climbed from the hole.

He patted his coat, until he found a black hole in the sleeve, which the bullet had made. He whistled and cursed. Then he picked up his revolver.

Jack expected Jukes to shoot him. But Jukes seemed impressed by his experience.

After a moment, he said, "It's late. I need to see my way back."

Jukes made Jack put back on his blindfold. He made Jack follow him back to the kauri grove, by ear. Jukes walked quietly, to train Jack's hearing, but he couldn't keep himself from humming.

"Follow me exactly. *Hmm?*" Jukes said. "Or else be sucked into the bog."

Jack tripped and fell, several times. Jukes kept humming, and Jack followed the humming. By the time they got back to the grove, Jack had learned how to walk lightly, and sightless.

It was like seeing with his ears. It was like reaching with his feet. Jack was feeling his way across the land. He began to appreciate it.

Then Jukes ripped off Jack's blindfold. Jack was standing in front of the open cellar door. Jack began to step down into it, but Jukes spun him around. His left eye looked wild.

"I have more to show you," he said. He pushed Jack backward, down into the cellar. He slammed the door shut, above him.

"Find some dinner," Jukes called down, through the door. "Get some sleep. I'll come for you when I'm ready."

48

When Jack did not return, Moxie tried to be a good leader, even though she felt dejected and miserable. She had the sheep dogs stand guard. They moved the sheep to a new pasture. They moved the sheep back. Days passed. More days passed. They waited for something to happen.

But because Jack was not there and the fangos did not attack, no sheep were killed and the sheep dogs had no food.

Hunger gnawed at their insides. Their ribs began to show again. The sheep dogs lost their energy and their sense of purpose.

All except Blur, whose purpose it was to keep going to the top of the sea cliffs to chase bird shadows.

Finally, Moxie went to tell him to come down and help guard sheep. If the sheep dogs were all going to starve, Moxie thought they should starve working together.

Blur was at the cliff top, set in his stance, quivering and expectant, waiting for a bird shadow to chase across the meadow.

"It's time you acted like a sheep dog," Moxie told him.

Blur didn't look up. His tail kept wagging.

"Blur," Moxie said.

"Blur," she repeated.

But Blur was spellbound. It made Moxie even sadder that the only happy dog on the island was happiest when he was chasing a shadow.

At that moment, a bird shadow came across the ground. Blur spotted it and was after it, dashing full speed. *Zip! Zoom!* He ran as fast as the bird above him, as it glided on gray wings down the slope of the meadow.

Moxie watched for Blur to trip and tumble. She waited for him to crash into a big rock. But Blur was able to run full speed, with his nose right on top of the gliding bird's shadow.

The bird paid Blur no attention as it slipped through

the air. It coasted, with Blur right below it, tearing through the bushes. Then the bird veered right, toward a grassy mound near where Mother Molly was sheltering her puppies.

It happened so fast that Moxie didn't catch it all. And who knew? Perhaps the bird was planning to swoop low, to scoop up some sheep's wool to use in its nest. Or perhaps it wasn't planning anything except flying, which birds can do easily without a plan.

But regardless of what was going through the bird's mind at this moment, it flew right over the grassy mound, with Blur racing right beneath it.

Blur was running so fast that when he got to the mound, he ran right up its side and into the air. And—

Fwop! Blur collided with the bird.

Squawk! Chomp! Blur bit the bird.

Blur slammed into the bird and his teeth chomped down on it. Blur fell to the ground with the bird still in his mouth. He got right up, and shook his ears, hard. That shook the bird, too, which killed it, if it wasn't already dead.

All the sheep dogs had witnessed Blur's great achievement—Moxie from the cliff's edge, Molly with her puppies, and Cam and Boffo and the other sheep dogs around the flock. All saw Blur's feat, and all were amazed.

"Blur!" Moxie barked. She ran down to him. The other dogs came down from the flock to crowd around him. Something tremendous had just happened.

"Fantastic! Did you see that?"

"I saw it!"

"Blur, can you do it again?"

Blur looked like he didn't know what it was that he had done. But he laid the prize at Molly's feet.

"Thank you," Molly said. She gave the bird to the puppies. They were now old enough to eat meat.

But the sense of celebration did not last long. One seagull was not enough even for the puppies. The sheep dogs and Moxie returned to the flock, to guard the sheep in the empty hollow of their hunger.

49

Jack lost his sense of how much time was passing. Then, one night, the cellar door swung open. Blackburn Jukes stepped down into Jack's dungeon, swinging a lantern.

Jack was lying back in a corner, where he had been sleeping under the Ecuadoran flag. With blinking eyes, Jack watched Jukes as he swung around his lantern. Jukes spied Jack. He marched over, and he grabbed Jack by the collar of his shirt. Without speaking, Jukes dragged Jack across the cellar floor, up the steps, and outside.

Jukes pushed Jack in front of him to the largest kauri tree, where the *Verboden* door was wide open and the orange light of kerosene lamps shone out. Jukes pushed Jack through the door and inside the tree.

Inside, the tree house was much bigger than it seemed from the outside. The ground-floor room was empty and as round as a pumpkin. Its wall was the varnished golden wood of the tree. Stair steps were pegged into the wall in a rising spiral. Jukes pushed Jack toward the stairs, and Jack climbed them to the second floor, where Scorch the cat hissed as soon as he saw him.

The upper room had the one crooked window that Jack had seen earlier. It was furnished with two chairs, a round table, and three rings of shelves. There were strange things on the shelves. But Jukes spun Jack around, and sat him down, into a chair at the table.

Jukes pressed Jack down by his shoulders. He was humming. He looked gripped by some thought.

"*Hmm?*" He said, "Welcome to my—*hmm?*—my factory?"

Something was going on with Jukes this night. His left eye was opened wider. His right eye seemed more dim.

"Yes, factory," Jukes said, again, as if this were the first time he'd thought of it. "This is my factory—of ideas."

Blackburn Jukes took a coil of wires from the shelf and placed it on his head.

"My thinking hat," he announced as he sat down in the other chair.

Jukes's left eye gleamed. His right eye glinted. He took out a match and scratched its head with his thumbnail, causing a thin thread of yellow smoke to rise from the match. Jukes sniffed in the yellow smoke like it was a thread of spiderweb.

"Ahh," he said. "That goes well."

Jukes's mind drifted, like the smoke, then his attention revived.

He held up a finger. "Watch this," he said.

He placed his fingertip next to his dull right eye. Then he pushed it into the eye socket. And he popped out his eye.

He caught it in his left hand.

Jack recoiled. "Hey!" he said.

Jukes's right eyelid was now closed. It was puckered and sunken. Jukes shrugged. He tapped the eye on the table, as if cracking an egg. "It is glass," he said. "But watch this."

He held the eye between his two hands. Then he unscrewed it into two halves.

"Voilà!" he said. "This shell has no nut. Or, not yet—"

Jukes reached into his vest pocket. He pulled out the small piece of amber that he'd displayed to Jack and Cookie on board the *Pym*. And he rubbed the amber until it glowed.

Jukes dropped the amber into one half of the glass eyeball. He screwed the eye back together. Then he pressed it to his empty eye socket, and popped it into place with the heel of his hand.

Jukes bent over his knees and adjusted his eye. He sat back up, blinking. The eye looked practically ablaze.

"Ha-hah!" Jukes said, beaming. "Look at me now!"

Jukes gazed around the tree house. His head was a human flashlight. He shone his light beam on Scorch the cat, and the cat arched his back.

Jack began to feel sorry for him. *He is mad,* Jack thought.

But Jukes slammed the table with his fist.

"I am sane!" he thundered.

Then Jukes's glass eye glowed even brighter. The humming began. It was the buzz-humming that Jack had first heard from Jukes, on board the *Pym*. But now it was louder and lower. It filled the tree house with a swelling vibration. Jack quaked with it. He buzzed with it. He quickly went so numb that he felt nothing at all, except the buzz.

Then Jukes snapped his fingers, to stop it. It left Jack senseless. He was numb. He thought he was deaf.

But Jukes whispered, and his voice sounded like it was inside Jack's head. He whispered, "It is an odd fact of science that children best hear my frequency of tone. If I had an army of children diggers, I could command them all."

He smiled at Jack. "You will find me more amber. You will dig me more amber until I have it all."

Then Jukes took Jack back to the cellar and locked him inside.

50

After that, Jack saw no light for several more days, except for the moments when Jukes lifted the cellar door and tied on Jack's blindfold. Over time, he learned the cellar by heart, much as he had learned to plumb the bog for amber. By touch, smell, sound, and feel, he knew the whole place. He thought of the little blind man on board the *Pym* who had told him to look, to find other ways to see.

Jack found food. He found fuel. He found a stove. But he found no matches. So he ate his tinned beef and crackers cold. He chased them down with handfuls of peanuts. All his food was salty, and his thirst was great.

He found an iron pipe, sticking out from the cellar wall. It dripped good cold springwater. So Jack put a bucket under the pipe to hold the water. There, he slaked his thirst and took his blind baths.

Jack got so good at seeing without using his eyes that he began to grow confident. He thought that if he could do almost anything blind, he ought to be able to escape. He tried digging his way out, but the kauri roots were so interwoven into the cellar's walls that digging out would have taken many months.

So Jack hit upon another scheme. In the cellar was a powder that he had first thought to be black pepper, but that turned out to be gunpowder. Jack thought first that he ought to be able to build himself a gun so he could shoot Blackburn Jukes, and escape.

But a gun seemed impossible to build in the dark with the materials he had. So Jack imagined he could build himself a cannon. For the cannon's barrel, he could use a leg from the old suit of armor.

"Amber cannon, my iron leg!" Jack joked to himself, chuckling.

He thought he could fill the barrel with gunpowder and the broken shards of the colored glass lampshades.

And when Jukes opened the cellar door one fine morning—

Ka-booom!

Jack smiled at the thought, although he knew that killing wasn't right.

He also knew that if he missed Jukes with his cannon, Jukes's pistol had six bullets.

Then Jack remembered how Jukes always wanted to get off the bog before nightfall. But for Jack, day and night were not any different. Jack no longer needed light.

So all Jack had to do was to make himself a good bomb. He could put it against the dungeon door, light its fuse, and—

Ka-booom!

If Jack blew out the door on a dark enough night, he could escape, and Blackburn Jukes couldn't follow. Jack could run back to Moxie. Together, they could live free.

51

Days passed. Things were going from bad to worse for the sheep dogs. They were starving. They couldn't kill a sheep and remain true sheep dogs. But if they didn't eat, they would die.

Growing desperate, Moxie decided to consult the scents of blind Sage and brave Kelso. Maybe they could tell her what to do in these dreadful times.

So Moxie went back to the old rock wall. She scratched at the ground, and sniffed. Finally, she dug up two faint scents, which smelled like they might hold memories. She stuck her muzzle into the dirt and inhaled of them all she could.

With a shimmer, both Sage and Kelso's visions appeared before her.

This excited Moxie. But the great dogs' visions remained dim. They looked like dreams of dreams.

"What do we do?" Moxie asked the visions. "What can we sheep dogs do?"

She had to sniff the dirt again to keep their visions intact.

Then, for the first time ever, Sage and Kelso spoke at the same time.

And for the first time, they seemed to say the same thing.

But their message was faint. Moxie could not quite make it out.

Either they both said, *Beware the fangos.*

Or they both said, *Be aware of the fangos.*

Then Sage and Kelso shimmered away, together.

They left Moxie standing alone, near the rock wall. She scratched at the dirt, but this time, nothing was there. Moxie padded back across through the meadow, to the sheep and the sheep dogs. There, she stood thinking for a long time, wondering and worrying over what she had been told.

Beware the fangos. That had always been Kelso's advice.

But *Be aware of the fangos?* What could Kelso and Sage have meant by that?

Beware. Or *be aware?* Moxie pondered and wondered, until she could wonder no more.

Moxie decided. She would become *aware* of the fangos. That had to be what the visions had meant.

Moxie took off running, down the meadow to the forest. She was going to find the fangos. She was going to face them, and be aware of them, in some way that she had not been before.

But lo, the fangos were gone. They were not lurking right inside the dark edge of the forest. They weren't sleeping under the dead leaves in their deadly, dark clearing. Moxie cast about the clearing, scratching the ground and sniffing, before she found a strong scent trail left by the fangos.

The trail led away, downhill. Moxie followed it at a run.

The fangos' scent trail led Moxie down through the forest and into a brushy ravine. She recognized this place. She had been there, many times in the past.

Then the scent trail led Moxie out the bottom of the ravine and onto a broad beach. It led her along the beach, past the huge rocks that reminded her of big dogs look-ing out to the sea. The path led her past the big rocks to below the high sea cliffs, which rose straight up to the meadow.

Moxie had been here, on this stretch of beach, too. This was where she had always gone to look for humans, and where she had first discovered Jack, more than a year before. It was also where Kelso and the fangos' leader had fallen, after the battle on the cliff top.

But Moxie wasn't looking for a human this time, or for the body of Kelso. She was looking for fangos. She kept to their scent trail, and followed it along the edge of the surf, and into an area of big jumbled boulders.

There, Moxie began to smell something . . . other. It smelled terrible, but it didn't smell bad like a fango did. It smelled dead.

Moxie slowed to a dogtrot. When she sensed she was near to the source of the odor, she jumped up onto a large boulder to get a wider view.

On the other side, Moxie saw them, the seven dire fangos. They were gathered around something in the sand. It was wet and black. It looked to be the remains of a seal. Most likely, the seal had been bitten by a shark, and had died and then washed ashore. Here, on the beach, the seal's carcass had rotted. The stench of it made Moxie gag.

Moxie swallowed back her disgust. She barked at the fangos.

The fangos looked up from their meal.

Moxie barked, and barked, and barked, at them.

"Follow me! Follow me!" she barked. "You must go back to your clearing!"

The fangos watched Moxie. Then they looked at one another.

Moxie jumped down off the boulder. She barked one more time, then ran back up the beach toward the ravine.

Be aware of the fangos, Moxie was thinking. How would she do that? She would be aware of their situation, and aware of their needs. Moxie would help the fangos.

52

Jack had started building his bomb as soon as he thought of it.

In the dark of the cellar, he rolled a big ball of gunpowder and some dry chaff, which he took from the barrel of peanuts. He packed all this, tight, inside a coating of mud. He made the bomb like the bombs he had seen in the comic pages in the newspapers. Then he sprinkled gunpowder onto a scrap of old silk and rolled it into a fuse.

Although he could not see it, Jack thought his bomb was a beauty—all round and heavy in his hands. Jack grinned like the bomb makers he had seen in the funny papers. They always grinned like they were crazy but happy.

Jack needed a way to light the bomb's fuse. But he had no matches or fire. He thought of a magnifying glass, but there was no sunlight coming into the cellar to focus on the fuse. Besides, Jack wanted to blast his way out of the cellar during a dark night, so a magnifying lens would not work.

Jack had to think for a few days before he hit on a notion. He remembered how the electricity had flowed all over Jukes when Jukes had rubbed the amber globe in the bog. Could Jack make electricity by rubbing the smaller amber globe that was in the cellar? Could he turn that electricity into a hot spark to ignite the fuse on his bomb?

"Yes, I could," Jack told himself.

He found the amber globe on the bench near the back of the cellar. He began rubbing it in his hands. Sure enough, he generated enough static electricity to make it begin to glow. He could feel the hairs begin to stand out on his arms. A copper-penny taste dripped down the sides of his tongue.

Holding the charged amber, Jack held his finger near the iron water pipe stuck into the wall of the cellar. *Zzzzt!* A spark jumped from his fingertip to the pipe.

"Aha!" Jack said. He had what he needed. He would not have to wait long.

The next day, as Jack was plunging a pole into the bog, Blackburn Jukes remarked on the weather. "There will be no moon tonight. No stars, either, because all will be cloudy. I'd hate to find myself alone on this bog. You'll be getting off work early today, my lad."

But Jukes made Jack work harder and faster than usual. Jack didn't mind. He had decided tonight was the night he would bolt.

The day's work passed. Jukes returned Jack into the cellar. In the pitch black of his dungeon, Jack waited until he was sure Jukes would be asleep in the tree house.

Then Jack took his handmade bomb to the locked cellar door. He wedged the bomb into the door's seam, away from the hinges. He straightened out the fuse, to make sure he had time to get away, before the bomb blew.

Jack pierced the end of the fuse with some copper wire and pushed the wire into the dirt floor to make sure it was electrically grounded. Then he went back into the cellar and got the amber globe.

Jack began to rub the globe. He rubbed it in a circular motion with the flat of his hand, trying to generate as much electricity as he could. Rubbing the globe reminded Jack of the old story of Aladdin and his magic lamp. He remembered that Aladdin, too, had been in a cave. Jack silently made a wish as the globe began to glow. He spit and stamped his foot so that his wish would come true.

Then Jack held his fingertip near the wire sticking through the fuse. A spark arced from his finger to the wire.

The fuse ignited.

"Oh, boy!" Jack said.

The fuse sputtered into flame. It looked like a Fourth of July sparkler.

"Ha ha!" Jack laughed. "Ho, ho!"

In the light from the fuse, Jack took one quick look around his prison of a cellar. He was surprised by all the garbage he had produced, lying around.

But then the sparks started gushing out of the end of the fuse. Jack had put too much gunpowder into it. The fuse began to flop around on the cellar floor. It was burning too quickly. It jumped like a loose fire hose on a ship's deck. It sprayed Jack with sparks. The flame raced up the fuse.

"Oh, no!"

All that Jack had time to do was to scuttle backward on his hands and bottom—

KA-BOOOOM!

53

Moxie had raced to the meadow and the hungry sheep dogs. She knew what she must do now, but she could not yet make herself do it. As the hungry sheep dogs watched her, she ran around and around the sheep, until she had herded them into a tight, bucking bunch.

But Moxie couldn't yet do what she knew she had to do. So she kept the sheep in a tight bunch well into the night. She worked like a sheep dog gone crazy, bullying the sheep. They bucked and they milled, but they obeyed her.

The sky was cloudy, dark. No stars. No moon. Moxie felt the need to howl, but since there wasn't a moon, she couldn't find her voice.

It made her all the more anxious. Moxie knew what she had to do. But she couldn't get started by herself.

Finally, past midnight, something pushed her to do it.

It was a faint noise in the distance.

Ka-boo-oo-oom—

Its echoes washed back and forth through the meadow.

—oo-oo-oo-oom—

The noise echoed through Moxie's brain as well.

She did not know what the sound was, but she felt it meant something—about Jack.

And it set Moxie to work.

54

B-b-b-brrzhh-z-z-z-z-z-z-zing-ng-ng-ngg!

Jack's ears were still ringing as he regained conscious-
ness. He lay flat on his back. His face felt like it was on
fire. He dabbed at his face with his fingers. It felt numb.

He stood, and started coughing, in thick and acrid
smoke. Hacking, he staggered backward and caught his
feet in the flag. He kicked the flag away, but he tripped
over the suit of armor. Jack pitched to his knees and
started to get back up. But he realized the air was better
nearer the floor. Jack crawled on his belly, until he got to a
cellar wall. Then crept his way along the wall to the door.

There, fresh air washed his face. *Ah!* The door was
gone! The way out was open. Happy, Jack stood up, into
the doorway.

He was free. He almost jumped up the steps. He stood still for a moment. Free! What a feeling. And yet—

And yet—?

And yet, this fact was strange. Jack could not see any kind of light.

Jack shook the thought from his mind. He breathed in good air, in big, gulping breaths. Before Jukes came to see what had happened, Jack would have to leave quickly.

But Jack's ears were still ringing. So he waited until the ringing passed. Meanwhile, Jack rejoiced in breathing the clean air. After the ringing had cleared, he reveled in the silence. It sounded plain and empty, but full of promise and hope. Jack touched his face again. Some feeling was coming back to it. That was good. He was OK. It was time to flee.

But something else stopped him. Jack listened. The silence had been replaced by the crunch and shuffle of footsteps. And a low humming.

It was a humming that Jack knew too well.

It was Blackburn Jukes.

"Hmmmm?" buzzed Jukes. He sounded near enough to touch.

And he was. His rough hand grabbed Jack by the shirt.

"*Hmm?*" Jukes said. "Just stepping out? *Hmm?* You broke the door? *Hmm?* You've made a mess of things, Jack. Including yourself. Here, let's take a look."

Jack felt the heat from a torch. But he could not see the flame.

"*Hmm,*" Jukes hummed.

Beside the humming, Jack heard a hiss from Jukes's cat.

Then Jukes whispered. "*Gadzoonds!*"

Jack felt the torch's heat go down his face's left side, then up the right side. Still, Jack saw no light.

"*Hmm, hmm.*" Jukes's hum sounded as if Jukes was shaking his head. "Your eyes are swollen shut," Jukes said.

Jukes laughed. "But that's good. With any luck, I'll never have to blindfold you again. I'll have me another blind digger!"

"You will *not*—!" Jack shouted. He tried to rub his eyes, but they hurt and he stopped.

Jukes laughed louder. And louder.

Jack waited. When it sounded like Jukes was laughing straight up to the sky, Jack took off, running, straight for the bog.

After Moxie had heard the big, faint boom wash through the night meadow, she had made one last circle around the flock of sheep.

Then she jumped onto the back of a sheep and began leaping from one sheep to another, all around the flock.

Moxie jumped, and she jumped, from one sheep to another, until she had landed on or had touched every sheep in the flock. She knew that she had to choose one sheep to cut out of the flock. But she was trying for some way for the choice to be made for her.

Suddenly, one sheep broke away from the flock. Moxie jumped down and ran after it. In a short space, she caught up with it. She ran alongside it, to turn it. She started the sheep running downhill through the meadow, in the darkness, toward the darker woods and the fangos.

56

Jukes shouted, "Stop!"

Jack ran.

Jukes yelled, "I'll shoot!"

But Jack ran.

Blam! Whzzzhhrrrrrr! A bullet zipped past Jack's ear.

Jack stopped and crouched. He blinked, but he still couldn't see. He touched his face, to feel his swelling and blisters. His eyelashes were crusted, his eyelids glued shut.

He needed to get a sense of direction, but Jukes shouted another curse. He was getting nearer. Jukes was coming Jack's way, crashing through the bushes. Echoes of the crashing bounced off tree trunks around Jack.

Jack swallowed. *Okay, okay, okay!* he thought. *What to do?*

Jukes shouted another curse. He was nearer yet. It sounded like he was whacking his torch against the trunks of the trees.

There was a *whack!*, then smaller echoes from all around Jack. Another *whack!*, then echoes: *crick, crack, scrack.*

As Jack listened to the echoes, he realized that they were making a sound image of the woods around him. If he listened carefully, he could hear where the trees were.

He could also hear where the trees were not.

Suddenly, Jack knew what to do.

He jumped up. He waved his arms.

"Can't catch me!" he shouted.

Bam! Whzhhrrrrrr! came a shot and bullet.

Jack ducked and listened. The sound of the shot was followed by echoes.

Jack listened. He heard where the trees were and were not. Even better, when a distant, loud echo returned, seconds later, Jack could hear the shape of the hills beyond the trees. With his hearing, Jack could feel where the gap and the trail were.

"Aha!" Jack shouted. He ran toward the gap.

Bam! Whzhhrrrrrr!

Then, echoes.

Bam! Whzhhrrrrrr!

More echoes.

Bam! Whzhhrrrrrr!

Jack ran.

Jukes cursed. Jukes fired.

Guided by the echoes, Jack ran between the trees and around the bog. Jack kept moving.

When Jukes quit his shooting, Jack started shouting short, sharp barks so he could hear echoes bounce off trees and rocks in front of him. He knew Jukes could follow, by listening for Jack's barks, but that didn't matter, right now.

Jack made it to the gap in the hills, and he found the trail that would lead him up toward the meadow. Jack knew where he was. He just couldn't see it.

He kept moving. Meanwhile, behind him—but never far enough—Jack heard Jukes occasionally shout.

In the dark of the night and in the depth of his blindness, Jack moved through the forest, sometimes stumbling, but always certain.

57

In the dark, Moxie herded the chosen sheep through the meadow. She guided it down to the black line of trees. When they reached the forest, the sheep balked. It refused to enter. But this had to be done. Moxie kept working at the luckless animal, until moved it along.

Inside the forest, Moxie immediately sensed the fangos. She stopped, and let the sheep trot ahead. She heard a sharp *bleat!*, a short scuffle, and then nothing. Moxie shivered, although the night was warm. She turned back, and went to wait in the trees near the edge of the meadow.

She felt beyond terrible. But it had to be done. Moxie felt that if the fangos were fed, then they would get stronger. If the fangos were stronger, they would start attacking the sheep again. And the sheep dogs would have a purpose in defending the sheep.

It could be the way it was—balanced—before Jack ever came to the island. The lives of the sheep dogs would be normal.

Moxie sighed. She laid her chin between her paws. It might be normal, but it would never feel natural without the presence of a human. And Moxie herself could never feel like a true dog, without her boy Jack beside her.

Moxie felt the dark of the night and the depths of her dog soul. She waited for the fangos to finish their meal. A wave of fatigue washed through her, and made her fall asleep.

Inside his blindness, Jack continued his running, always heading for the meadow and—he hoped—Moxie.

At last, he had to stop for rest, but as soon as his breathing subsided, Jack began to hear the noises made by Jukes. From below and behind him, Jack heard curses and shouts, and the sounds of stubborn anger. Blackburn Jukes was resolute.

Jack took a big breath, and continued up the hill. He barked and listened for the tree echoes to guide him. He could not see that the sky was getting lighter.

59

Moxie opened her eyes. The sky was lightening toward dawn. But she sensed something else had changed around her.

She had been surrounded by the fangos. Moxie startled upon seeing them. Her coat bristled. Her throat growled. She stood, and turned in a circle.

What now? she wondered.

The fangos watched her, with their blank fango expressions.

What now? What now would the fangos do? Moxie's lip curled in a snarl. She crouched, ready to fight.

One of the fangos stepped toward her. Then he stopped. He was the largest of the fangos, but even on his big frame, his newly filled belly looked round and swollen.

He lowered his head, and narrowed his eyes in con-
centration.

"*D-d-d-d*—" the fango began. "*D-d*—"

He was trying to communicate.

"*D-d-d-d-dog,*" he said. "*Y-y-ou. D-d-dog.*"

Moxie nodded. *Yes?* she wondered.

The fango nodded as well.

"*Uh—uh—us. F-f-f-f-f*—" he started. "*F-f-f-f-f*—"

But he could not finish.

"You are fangos." Moxie said it for him.

The fango winced. The name hurt him. He shook
his head.

"*Uh—uh—us. F-f-f-fan-g-gos,*" he said. "*Uh-uh-us.
F-f-fed.*

"*F-f-fed,*" he said, again. "*Th-th-th—Th-th-than-
n-g-k*—"

"Thank you?" Moxie offered.

The fango's eyes brightened.

"*Th-th-thang*—" he tried to say.

Moxie was amazed. Something huge had changed,
here. Who knew what might happen—and what changes
might come?

"*W-w-we-ee w-wannuh b-be-ee d-d-d*—"

"You want to be *dogs?*"

But suddenly Moxie lifted her nose. She smelled something else, on the breeze. Another change was in the air. She looked back at the fango.

"Come with me!" Moxie said to him.

"Come with me!" she told all of the fangos. "And be dogs."

At last, Jack realized that he had made it to the meadow. The place sounded open—wide and high. There were no more echoes to bounce back to him and help him find direction. But he knew if he headed uphill, he would arrive at the sheep dogs.

He laughed. He started running. He began to run with abandon. Again and again, he tripped over tussocks and rocks. He fell and rolled. He got up, laughing. Jack kept falling and getting up, running and laughing.

When Jack got to the top of meadow, he stumbled straight into the flock of sheep. The sheep maaed and moved away, but Jack grabbed their fleeces and hugged them. He loved the dirty, smelly, woolly sheep.

He whistled for the sheep dogs. He sat down in the

grass. He hugged and he kissed each of the sheep dogs as they came up to him and touched their noses to his hands.

Jack couldn't see them, but he recognized them by their sizes and by the feel of their coats. "Cam! Boffo! Tram!" Mother Molly's puppies tumbled into Jack's lap.

But where was Blur? "Blur!" Jack called. Blur was not there. Of course, Blur was often not near.

"Moxie!" Jack shouted. "Moxie!"

Moxie was not there, either.

"Where is she, gang?" Jack kept asking the sheep dogs. "Where is my Moxie?"

Jack waited. But Moxie was not there.

Jack remained sitting on the ground as the puppies played in his lap. What had become of Moxie, since that day that Jukes had thrown Jack into the cellar?

Jack rubbed his swollen eyes. He had to see! He rubbed at them, hard, until he heard a sheep dog growl.

It was a low growl. It said, *There's a threat!*

"What is it, Cam?" said Jack.

Cam growled again.

Then Jack heard a hiss.

"Oh, no!" It was a cat.

"G-r-r-r-r!" Cam growled again.

"H-s-s-s-s!"

Then Jack heard heavy breathing, the rasps of a man heaving for breath.

Needless to say, it was Blackburn Jukes.

Jack sat still, waiting. There was nowhere to run. It took a minute for Jukes to catch his breath. Then he coughed. He cleared his throat. He began to hum.

"Huh-huh-hmmmmmm—" Jukes began.

Jack covered his ears, but it was no use.

"Hmmm-mbzzzzz—" The hum gained in volume. Then it added the buzz.

"Hmmbbzzzzzzzzz—"

And louder. *"BBBZZZZZZZZZ—"*

Jack stuck his fingers in his ears, but his cheeks began to buzz. The buzzing ran down his neck and out his arms.

"BBZZZZZZZ—" Jukes's buzz filled his brain.

Jack was about to scream, but Jukes broke down and started coughing.

Hacking and spitting, Jukes fell into a coughing jag. Jack pulled his head down between his shoulders to try to avoid the spatter.

Finally, Jukes's spasms stopped.

"Curse it!" he said. He coughed again, although more lightly. "But curse it. Curse it. No matter. I'll remaster you, young Jack, back at the cove."

Then Jukes muttered to himself, pensively, for a few moments.

Even in his blindness, Jack felt Jukes's eyes staring at him. Jack could not bear it. He could not help himself. He felt himself begin to cry. Tears welled up inside his crusted eyelids. Jack tried not to sob. He cried in little squeaks.

Jukes tsked him with his tongue. "Oh, the poor boy in the meadow. And—*oh!*—of all the pitiful sights— of which I have seen many. I swear that I have. But, clearly, you really should *see* yourself, Jack, in the light of this day."

Jukes tried humming again. But he coughed, then he chuckled. "But, of course, you can't see yourself, can you, my lad?"

Jack sniffed, and said nothing.

Jukes heaved a dramatic sigh. Then he laughed his stage laugh. "Ha-ha-ha! Ha-ha-*hah*! *Hah-ha-ha-ha-ha!*" His laughter subsided to chuckles.

"Nice pasture you have up here," he said finally. "You know, I could use a little mutton, to go with my tinned cabbage. But we can come back up for that later. *Eh,* Jack? Until then, my small friend—"

Jukes rustled with something in his coat pockets. Jack heard Jukes step nearer. Then he smelled Jukes's breath on his face.

"First things first," Jukes said.

Jack startled as something dropped over his head.

It tightened around his neck. Jack grabbed it. It was a rope. Jack tried to pull it away from his throat.

"No!" he pleaded. "No! Mr. Jukes! Mr. Jukes! Please!" Jack put his hands together, as in prayer. "Please. Don't hang—!"

"Oh, quiet!" Jukes ordered. "It just feels like a noose. But it's your new leash, Jack. You might say it's your new *leash on life.* And—*Oho!* I'm going to keep you on a short leash, from now on. *Hmm?* All right, then. Let us go back down to our bonny amber bog."

Jack's shoulders slumped. He felt Jukes flip the leash.

"Giddyup, boy!" Jukes whistled and clucked his tongue.

Jack rose to one knee. He felt bowed and beaten. But he had one good thought in his mind.

Moxie. Where was she? *Where* was she?

Then Jack detected the rumbling of feet, running. It was a rolling, rumbling drumming, coming along the ground. It was coming nearer. And closer.

And what? Was it Moxie? Jack rubbed at his eyes.

The cat hissed. Then it screeched.

"*R-r-r-reee-er-rrr!*"

Jukes shouted, "What the blazes—?"

Then—*WHUMP!*

"Ooof!"

Something had hit Jukes. Jack heard him *thump* to the ground. He rubbed at his eyes.

"Curse it!" Jukes swore.

Jack heard Jukes trying to stand. Jack rubbed at his eyes.

Then Jukes cried, "What in the bla—?"

WHUMP!

"Ooof!" Jukes fell again.

Jack jumped up. He shouted, "Blur?"

It had to be Blur!

Jack listened with all his might. He heard Blur coming back.

The drumming got closer. Jack expected another *whump!*

Instead, he heard, *BLAM!*

Jack's ears rang. Then silence filled his head.

Seconds later, a gunshot's echo rolled past.

Then, silence again. Sharp gunpowder smoke stung in Jack's nose.

"Blur?" asked Jack. His voice quavered.

"Blur?" *Oh, no!* Had Jukes had just shot Blur?

"Oh, no!" Jack rubbed at his eyes. He had to see! He blinked. He rubbed his eyes again, harder and harder. He grabbed handfuls of dewy grass and rubbed them on his eyes.

Jukes was muttering. "You miserable, miserable cur! You just try it. Just try it. You come at me again."

Jukes must have missed. Blur was alive! Jack clapped his hands in thanks. He saw a patch of light. Jack blinked at it and rubbed his eyes again, but the light smeared into a smudge of green and blue.

"Blur! Watch out!" Jack shouted. He rubbed the grass against his closed eyes.

He heard a *click!*

Jack knew that Jukes had cocked back the hammer on his pistol.

"No!" Jack pleaded as he rubbed at his face.

Jukes was chuckling. "Eat this, you mongrel cur. One. Two. Three—"

CLACK.

Then silence.

Blackburn Jukes had run out of bullets.

61

Moxie and the fangos raced through the meadow.

They ran through the grass and tussocks, up toward the flock of sheep.

Ahead, Moxie saw the sheep dogs.

Then she saw Blur.

And then—?

Was it Jack?

Yes, there was Jack!

Moxie exulted. She leaped, and she leaped again, for joy.

But—wait! Why was Jack down like that, on one of his knees?

And who could that be, standing over him, there?

Moxie knew at once who it was. It was that bad man.

Moxie yipped. She ran harder. Running beside her, the fangos spread out.

The fangos knew what to do.

62

Jack heard a yip from down the meadow. He jumped to his feet.

"Moxie!" he shouted.

Jukes muttered, "What now? Now, what in blue blazes?"

Scorch the cat hissed. Two empty *clacks!* came out of Jukes's pistol. Jukes began to moan, in aggravation and terror.

Then Blackburn Jukes screamed. Jack heard him running away.

Jukes was gone!

Then Jack heard a rushing as several animals ran past him.

Then Jack felt a small dog jump up against him, again and again.

"Moxie! Moxie!" Jack laughed. "Moxie! Moxie!"

Jack held out his arms. Moxie leaped into them.

Jack sank to the ground as Moxie covered him with kisses. She licked his hands. She licked his face. She licked his eyes.

As she licked his eyes, she washed away the blinding crusts.

Light shone into Jack's eyes again.

The first thing Jack saw, of course, was Moxie.

"Love you!" Jack shouted.

But Jack had to see more. He needed to see what had happened to Blackburn Jukes.

Jack jumped up. Jukes was gone. All that remained was a pistol, lying in the grass.

Jack ran to the grassy mound where Mother Molly sheltered her pups. He scrambled to the top of it, and stood, scanning the meadow, below him.

Where was Jukes? Where?

There he was! Down below. Jukes was running for his life, being chased by the gang of fangos. His cat, Scorch, was riding on the top of his head.

"Oh, my!" Jack said, wincing at the sight. He cringed as he waited for the fangos to take Jukes down.

But they didn't. The fangos checked themselves. They broke off the chase at the forest's edge. They stopped and let Jukes run into the woods. Then they turned. They started loping up the slope, back toward Moxie and Jack.

"Moxie! Did you see that?" asked Jack of Moxie, who stood by him. "Those fangos. They are acting exactly like sheep dogs!"

63

Moxie, the little Border collie, trotted along the sea cliffs. She stopped and looked down across the grassy green meadow. Below her, Mother Molly was being teased by her puppies. Beyond them, the sheep grazed, tended by the sheep dogs.

Moxie saw Cam, Boffo, and Tram. With them, she saw the new herders, those who had once been fangos. They were now noble and honest sheep dogs.

All was well on the island. But where was Blur? Where was that Blur—*ever*?

As if in answer, Moxie heard two sounds. Both sounds were coming nearer.

She heard the *fw-fw-fw!* of the flying white stick that Jack had named *Blur Bird*.

She also heard the drumming rumble of Blur's feet across the ground.

Fw-fw-fw-fw!

B-b-b-l-l-r-r-r-r-rumble!

Moxie crouched lower as the sounds got louder and came together.

Suddenly, she saw the flying white stick, whirling above her.

At the same instant, she saw Blur in front of her as he leaped into space.

Snap! Blur snatched the flying stick out of the air. He spun away with it, and he crashed into a bush.

Then Moxie heard happy barking. It was Jack, running along the cliff top, waving his forelegs above his head.

"Hey! Hey! Moxie!" Jack was shouting as he came up to her. "Moxie. Did you see that? Ha-ha! Wasn't that great?"

They sat down together on the cliff top, facing the ocean. Jack hugged Moxie close to him, leaning his head against hers.